FURRY CREEK

Victoria
Feb. 28, 2000

To Helen,
with Best Wishes,
Keith

Furry Creek

by

Keith Harrison

OOLICHAN BOOKS
LANTZVILLE, BRITISH COLUMBIA, CANADA
1999

Canadian Cataloguing in Publication Data
Harrison, Keith.
   Furry Creek
ISBN 0-88982-182-8

   1. Lowther, Pat, 1935-1975—Fiction. I. Title.
PS8565.A656F87 1999   C813'.54   C99-910983-9
PR9199.3.H348F87 1999

We gratefully acknowledge the support of the Canada Council for the Arts for our publishing program.

THE CANADA COUNCIL | LE CONSEIL DES ARTS
FOR THE ARTS | DU CANADA
SINCE 1957 | DEPUIS 1957

Grateful acknowledgement is also made to the BC Ministry of Tourism, Small Business and Culture for their financial support.

We acknowledge the financial support of the Government of Canada through the Book Publishing Industry Development Program for our publishing activities.

Canadä

Published by
Oolichan Books
P.O. Box 10, Lantzville
British Columbia, Canada
V0R 2H0

Printed in Canada

To Jo

Acknowledgements

Although much use has been made of documents, all of the point-of-view characters (or what Henry James would call "sentient centres") are completely fictitious. In a few instances testimony from transcripts has been slightly edited, and sometimes it has been transposed from the preliminary hearing to the actual trial. Newspaper excerpts appear by permission of *The Vancouver Sun*.

Correspondence and essays from Beth and Christine Lowther reproduced in this book remain the copyright of the authors, and all rights to the poems by Pat Lowther included here are reserved to her Estate, whose permission is very gratefully acknowledged. Many of the poems reprinted can be found in Pat Lowther's *Time Capsule: New and Selected Poems* (Polestar, 1996), which offers a fine, representative gathering of her work. Another source has been *A Stone Diary* (Oxford, 1977), also a very strong collection. Several of the poems in *Furry Creek*, "Skin," "Division," and "These are our insufficient coins," have never been published before.

Thanks to Kate Braid for asking me to re-imagine some moments in my text, to Ron Smith for saying "yes" when this project was still full of question marks, and to Ursula Vaira for making many of the flaws disappear, as if by magic. Thanks to Rob Pettigrew for the cover image.

This book, inspired by Pat Lowther's art, could not have been written without the generous sharing by her children: Alan Domphousse, Kathy Lyons, Beth Lowther, and Christine Lowther.

This is the place
you would rather not know about,
this is the place that will inhabit you,
this is the place you cannot imagine

Margaret Atwood

"Notes Towards a Poem
That Can Never Be Written"

100

Yes he is full now
like an articulated shell,
fragile, enclosing liquid.
The slightest thing
brims his eyes:
any emotion
or a minute lapse
of memory, self-doubt;
his lips tremble
like black moths' wings,
his eyes blue
as watered milk startle
through lenses of tears.
He cannot speak
to you, to anyone,
without these tears
surprising him.
His hand inky with veins
falters towards your wrist,
your arm: touch
anchors him here, upright.
There is an urgent message
fluttering
like his pulse,
a prayer, a summation.
Always, from breath to breath,
he is saying goodbye.

• Pat Lowther

Saturday night, October 18, 1975

Had no time to make the drive from the coast through the Rockies. As a result of information, I attended by airplane. Mom reached me late, after I got back from Lion's Gate Hospital and that other body: "Stevie, he's decided to pack it in. You'd better get here quick. He won't eat anymore."

Home to Medicine Hat. Arrived too late. The pretty little faces of my sister's kids squashed against the glass, and Mom waiting by the open front door for a hug. Bronco Tom, dead at last.

Compassionate leave.

"What's the share of two birthday cakes for fifteen people?" he'd ask me. I'd never know the answer and wouldn't say nothing. Bronco Tom would soon give up on me and snort, "About as smart as a turnip." I attended, as a result of information.

Now, coming back in the night to the coast. Can't tell how fast this plane's moving, or where we are.

Just up in the air, next to the sleeping body of a stranger. If snow's down below, it looks black. Most of Canada so cold, a lot of empty land needed to keep life going. On my one overnight flight above the U.S., pockets of light every couple of minutes. Here, nothing for the eye to grab hold of. Been nearly half an hour out of Calgary airport, so we must have crossed the border into B.C. Might not catch any lights until Vancouver.

Can't see much on the coast a lot of the time, except rain and fog on top of a grey sea, or mountains that are in the way. Miss the big open prairie sky where you can look forever.

"Born a year or so after the last Ice Age scraped the prairies flat," Bronco Tom said. "Lassoed mammoths and mastodons."

Only scattered towns, like Medicine Hat, which seemed pretty little after Vancouver. The Hat. Where the good people from the Goodyear tire plant know the folks from Northwest Nitro Chemicals. Even with the hurried-up funeral, half the town managed to pay their respects. The prairie wind blowing all the time.

Saturday nights were like a scene from *American Graffiti*. Newly washed and polished cars cruising around and around the one downtown block that mattered. Boys with short hair and clean clothes from farms and ranches, riding in their dad's trucks, the chrome shined, and maybe a few day-glo paint-jobs. Lagging behind, then accelerating just for fun, an open case of beer handy, but semi-hidden. Girlfriends with shampooed hair squeezed next to the boys in the cab, even when a gear shift on the floor got in the way.

Everyone revving their engines, a few vehicles with mufflers perforated with a screw-driver for better sound effects. Gunning up to red lights, smirking at the "pigs" in the squad car who were usually smart enough to just stare straight ahead. Maybe by midnight some guys, their brains soaked with beer, would throw a punch or two, but all pretty harmless stuff. Not a battered head and bloated body in a river.

"Born in a log tent," Bronco Tom said. "Just two lean-tos pushed up against each other and chinked with mud and needlegrass. Lasted only a season. Called 'hog sties,'" he said. "Born in a manger," he yelped.

I'll never figure him out.

"Fought *alongside* the Blackfoot," he would tell me, with yips of laughter. "Born beside the South Saskatchewan River, in 1875, eight years *before* the railway got here. A medicine man sucked out all my illness when I was three. Later, the chief gave me a pair of black-dyed moccasins and sent me out on a vision quest, up into the Cypress Hills. Found a deck of cards."

Beneath his Stetson hat, a scam artist with blue eyes. Bronco Tom said that before The Great War, whenever he arrived in a strange town, he would walk into the nearest store, pick up some cheap item, like a package of pins, and place it on the wooden counter, alongside his uncreased twenty dollar bill. He would push and pull back that new bill so many times, put it down and pick it up while he looked in all of his different pockets, under his hat, and even inside a boot with its spur, holding it upside down and shaking, waiting for some coins to drop out. No one never suspected a cowboy had brains, he said. Stood there in a red wool sock. Finally, the distracted cashier gave him change for the twenty Bronco Tom had repocketed.

But after Vimy Ridge, he told me, he was a changed man.

In my very first Little League game, struck out twice, looking. Heard him yell from the stands: "The bat's not tired. Stop resting it on your shoulder." Scared at looking bad, I just hoped each pitch would be called a ball. But the next time up I swung at the first pitch with all my might and the ball shot down the third baseline. I ran, shocked and happy, all the way to second base. After the game, when I was climbing up into his truck, he tested me, "You went one for three. What's that as a percentage?"

Always spoiled my fun. .33333333333333 . . . The cut-off, totally arbitrary. The digits of a batting average forever incomplete. Like missing fingers on a hand, or a head with its ears torn off.

Bronco Tom lied about his age, he said, and enlisted in The Great War. Came back to Canada in 1918, carried from a troopship to the Halifax train station on a stretcher, but at Medicine Hat he limped off on crutches, stepping down one stair at a time to the platform, then pulled himself up into a horse and buggy, and went looking for a ranch to buy, cheap. Less than a week later Bronco Tom found the place, and a young woman from Seven Persons to marry him. She waited two days for a big windstorm to die down, then nodded yes. He chopped up his crutches, he said, for kindling.

Never asked granny why. The townsfolk whispered her intended had been in the Canadian Corps with Bronco Tom. Had given his life for his country, which was miles and miles of short brown prairie grass before the irrigation lines came from Grassy Lake.

The RCMP a bit like the military. Get to carry a gun, wear a badge, drive cars beyond the legal speed limit. Didn't want to be cooped up with sissy paperwork. Didn't want neither to find the fractured skull of a woman with no hair on its head.

When I proudly told grandpa I'd been accepted into the Royal Canadian Mounted Police, he said, "Pigs will eat anything, even rattlesnakes," and gave his little yelp. Mom's whole body went stiff with rage, "You apologize right now to Stevie, or I'm leaving your house." Bronco Tom just shuffled off to his bedroom. A minute or two later he came back out, carrying a pair of black moccasins. "Take them," he whispered. "You're a warrior now." Squeezed my hand so hard the knuckles hurt.

Arrived too late.

On Armistice Day, Bronco Tom would get into uniform, pressed by Mom the evening before, and march outside in boots he'd polished himself for twenty minutes. Always came home after dark. Last November 11th I got out of bed and found Bronco Tom sitting in blackness at the kitchen table. His blue eyes cringed when I turned on the light bulb. Started to cry, breathing beer fumes in my face, whimpering wisdom at me. "Only wishes are perfect. The world itself is shaped like one big fat zero. If you're lucky, all you get are some bits and pieces not worth measuring." Then why did he drive me half-crazy as a kid dividing everything up and figuring out percentages? Wanted to shout at him, but Bronco Tom in his faded uniform was already talking about Vimy Ridge.

"The British couldn't do it. The French couldn't do it. We guys in the Canadian Corps did it, all alone. We took Vimy Ridge from the Huns. Ignored the machine guns, and just walked straight up that god damn hill. Three thousand, five hundred and ninety-eight of us boys killed." So many lives, unlived.

Lying there in his coffin, Bronco Tom looked calm and friendly and handsome in a dim kind of way, like an older Gerald Ford.

Betty Ford didn't even know her husband had been shot at, that second time. Asked him innocently as she boarded Air Force One for their flight home, "Did you have a nice time?" First, Squeaky Frome, a Charlie Manson groupie, then Sally Moore, an overweight accountant from some rich family. The joke went around about Ford being such a useless president he couldn't even get a decent assassin. Women now out of control. That fugitive, Wendy Yoshimura, who plotted to bomb naval buildings. Arrested with Patty Hearst, who goes into a bank with a machine gun and, when she's booked, lists her occupation as "urban guerrilla." Denounces her parents as "pigs." What was it Bronco Tom said, when the drilling rigs started moving in? "Always has been lots of natural gas around."

Would be nice if my Betty were waiting at the Vancouver airport for me. Even with the padded armrest between us, her body shuddered against mine in the movie theatre. The Sheriff stared out at the sea where the girl swimmer had been eaten. Roy Scheider, with his broken nose, would get the one responsible. Just make-believe, but Betty said she would never ever go swimming again.

In my hip waders, searched west towards Howe Sound, then east of the railway trestle, but found nothing on neither bank. Only the body at the fork in the river. Placed a plastic baggie over one hand, then the other, and a much larger one for her head, then two more for the feet. Then the three of us lifted that more than human weight into a body bag. Out of Furry Creek, on Thanksgiving Monday.

Into the thin air. Only night outside this vibrating metal shell.

From the parking lot at Lion's Gate Hospital, where the ambulance took the dead woman, I stared out to sea at the red-orange sunset. That English guy doing the autopsy had three soft-rubber horseshoes as chins. Not worried, I guess, about his luck spilling out from all of them at once. Said some critic called it "a masterpiece of horror." What's his name? Clyde Gilmour. Remember the warning about no one being admitted during the last fifteen minutes. Mature. "Some frightening and gory scenes."

Never did see Bronco Tom cry. Until he was nearly a hundred. Not even at Dad's tractor accident. "A thing like this, can't never tell how you'll react." Couldn't never get that hurting tightness out of my chest.

Departing for Bronco Tom's funeral, I was afraid if

Betty's long arms let go of me I would end up on the airport floor, a puddle.

As a result of information, I attended. Approximately three hundred and fifty feet west of Highway 99, along the Furry Creek. Beyond the railway trestle. A nude body, in the fork of the river, face down among some rocks beneath a large cedar log. A number of birds around. Part of the skull was missing, and the ears were torn. There was no hair on its head. Couldn't tell the colour of the eyes.

This plane now being battered by rain.

Determined to get the killer. She could have been Betty.

Part of the hand in the water, white and shrivelled. The first body I went down close to, in the line of duty.

Dad's eyes were brown like wet prairie earth. That face I always loved, the son of Bronco Tom. Looking off into the horizon. His neck bent sideways. Always, saying good-bye.

Couldn't find nothing but bright air.

Cloud Horses

for Beth

In my daughter's dream
are black horses
and white horses;
she says there are
also cloud horses
for every colour of sky

Under her closed
eyelids her eyes move
following horses;
she will not say more,
she has decided to keep
her dreams private

She moves in sleep
and in the country
of her days where
i cannot follow:
i see her riding away
on a horse whose colour
i have no name for

• Pat Lowther

Wednesday early morning, April 14, 1976

Every time I wake in the dark.
Every night it starts with a young woman screaming. Her baby has been taken. I stumble out into a
long, shadowed hallway, along with other guests in a
run-down resort hotel. This stranger cries out as if
hot iron tongs pinch her flesh. Our faces mostly hidden, we stand in hospital gowns under dim ceiling
lights, watch her hit the small chained hammer against
the rounded glass. Soundlessly it shatters, and the fire
alarm starts a crazed ringing.
I touch my hand to her hot shoulder and my fingers catch on fire. Orange flames flare from my fingertips, but don't hurt. As we glide downstairs to the
lobby, I blow on them, until my hand looks like an
ashy candelabra.
All the doors are locked, the windows bolted. The
smiling chef wears a rust-spotted apron, leans on a

fireplace mantle above a mound of charcoal as high as my waist. The fire alarm quits its hellish ringing.

A red hole screaming, the young mother's voice begins again. She bunches up her sun-yellow gown, trying to wring herself out, knotting and squeezing all the colour from the cloth until it's just a wet, grey rag in my hand.

Sucking air in too quickly – not waiting to breathe out what's already in my lungs.

Sunset walks over my body. The stupid cat thinks it must be dawn because I've lifted my head from the damp pillow. Winded, my leg muscles tense, I feel like I've been kicking my way through very dense water.

I can sense my blood pressure ease as I pet Sunset's striped body. I ruffle the orange fur around his neck. His bony head nudges at me, trying to get me up. Sunset, you sure have bad breath. Due to gingivitis. Needs to rest his mouth after eating only a few bites of food. "Sunset, do you have a leaky tooth, a little abscess?" I'll have to make another appointment with the vet. "You purr boy."

He turns, ringed tail in the air. Stares at me with amber eyes: Get up, now, Angela. He steps all his weight down on my stomach, starts kneading me. Thinks I'm his mother.

I did buy him a finger brush and some cat toothpaste, but it hurt his gums too much when I tried it. Last night I couldn't find the energy to floss my own teeth. Fatigued, I guess, by an afternoon of testimony.

> Q   Now, do you recognize that particular
>   hammer, Exhibit Q?

A   *Yes, my initials appear on the handle.*

From nervous waiting, no saliva left in my mouth when I had to speak, officially.

A   *Forensic serology deals with the identi-fication of body fluids such as blood and seminal fluid.*

Not totally inept for my first court appearance, I guess.

Q   *Now, you are a civilian member of the Royal Canadian Mounted Police, correct?*

A   *Yes.*

Q   *And with respect to that, were you employed on October the 16th, 1975?*

A   *Yes, Sir I was.*

Q   *And where was that?*

A   *At the Crime Detection Laboratory in Vancouver.*

The early part of the testimony easy, rehearsed – almost felt like cheating, as if I had gotten hold of a copy of the exam questions beforehand.

"OW! Get your claws out of my flesh." He didn't mean to hurt me. "Retract." You can talk to a pet without feeling moronic the way you do when you talk out loud to yourself. Sunset, a typical guy, looks miffed at having to stop. Walks away stiffly to the foot of my bed.

Q   *And did you conduct an examination of that particular hammer?*

A   *Yes, I did.*

Q   *And what were your findings?*

A   *I found human blood of an insufficient quantity to group. I circled this area, and the area is between the head and the handle.*

Q   *Now you're showing us an area circled by what appears to be black ink, is that correct?*

A   *Yes.*

Q   *And that is on the side of the hammer that contains your initials.*

A   *That is correct.*

I'm definitely not going to get back to sleep. Always the fear next time I will not blink open my eyes and lash my body into consciousness, because that split second will take longer than I have left. Nearly an hour of our waking day, supposedly, spent with our eyes shut. That way we don't have to rinse out our eyes so much, or feel like we're crying all the time. Was I blinking on the witness stand?

Q   *And besides finding blood in that area, did you find blood on any other portion of that hammer?*

A   *Yes, I found blood of an indeterminate species origin on the claw.*

Q   *And which portion of the claw, underneath or on top of the claw?*

A   *Underneath.*

Q   *And you've told us that you can't even tell us if it's human blood, correct?*

A   *That is correct.*

Q   *And that is because of insufficient amount?*

A   *Yes.*

Sunset curves towards me and meows. "You want breakfast?" He bumps his stripey head against my hand. I know it's foolish to get up and feed him now because tomorrow he'll want to eat this early again. I have to go pee anyway.

Stepping onto the cold rug, I shiver. Sunset jumps down from the bed eagerly. Next to the light scattering of his claws, my feet pad heavily. His soft, purposeful life brushes warmly against my leg as I feel for the switch. I'm training my cat to wake me at 6:30 every morning, but his company is almost worth it.

Q   *And this blood, was it on the outside or was it in – in between the handle and the head?*

My black wet suit hangs in the shower stall, like a very unromantic date. A hood to hide my hair. The

23

gloves, the wide false face of the goggles, the hose dangling. The flippered booties look like water babies.

> Q   *Okay. Of all the areas you took samples, were there any areas that were not found to be human blood?*

> A   *No, Sir.*

Staggered, like that first time I had to lug the heavy tanks with their J-valves from the van to the shore. All that weight strapped in back of me. Needing to take quick, short steps to get my balance. Toppling over backwards into the lake water, straight down. Suddenly I found myself breathing underwater, rich oxygen air, free to explore deeper, going to the very bottom of the lake. But when you reach 500 p.s.i. in the tank, it feels like you're running out of air – a signal to put the valve up – and I forgot, or didn't care after the abortion. The weird laughing gas in my brain just bumped me down further. Not even worried as I slid another two or three fathoms deeper. Giggling until the end. At the lake's bottom, coldness cut right through my black wet suit.

I could climb back into my warm bed for another half hour.

There on the gravelly bed, dozens of leaves from a maple tree. Bright yellow and red, perfectly preserved.

> Q   *And did you find the reddish marks within the black circles there to contain human blood?*

> A   *Yes, they did.*

Q   Now I note that they appear to be circles with a clear centre.

A   Yes, Sir.

Q   On both photographs, is that correct?

A   Yes.

Q   And is it true that the edges of a drop of blood, for instance, will dry faster than the centre if it was thicker in the centre than at the edge?

A   Yes.

Q   And would you agree with me that if a person were to wipe an area such as that depicted . . . ?

Sunset has disappeared. Probably asleep on my warm pillow.

Waiting there on the gravelly bed, giggling.

Uncle Dave and Dad finally caught up to my descent, and one of them turned my J-valve up. Then I was rising too fassssst, in a dizzy panic, believing there was some malfunction of the tank. Brain-warped and coming up for air too soon, sputtering like some mindless toy in a bathtub. Dad, my buddy, held my legs tight, kept me down there, waited with me, adjusting to the pressure of less water above us. Holding my head intact.

Q   Now, the hammer, did you remove the head from the wooden handle?

A   No, Sir. No, I did not.

During cross-examination, I felt exposed, unprofessional.

Q   *You found in an area which you indicated was circled, where the handle joins the head of the hammer, that there was some blood in underneath the head, is that correct?*

A   *Well, not underneath. It was between the head and the handle.*

Q   *Well, would that be underneath the metal?*

A   *Well, it appears like the – the head is very tight on the handle. It would be just beside it.*

Endless discussion of blood.

Q   *All right. Well, –*

A   *It may appear like there's a lot of blood on a stain sometimes and yet it could be a very thin film.*

Q   *All right. Was it visible to the naked eye?*

A   *On the hammer?*

Q   *Yes.*

A   *I do not recall. However, I know I used the microscope to examine the hammer.*

Q *You don't remember whether you saw it with the naked eye before you used the microscope?*

A *No, Sir.*

My brain under the pressure of cross-examination nearly crushed, and yesterday was only the preliminary inquiry. Not the real trial. Recording all my words.

A *It's difficult to say just a drop of blood because the concentration varies so greatly.*

Finally, we reached the glittery surface. Uncle Dave gave me a thumbs-up sign and Dad had a tired smile. I could breathe air once more without a mouthpiece and a tank. On that shivery, sunny day, looking around the lake, I saw no trees anywhere close to the shore. All of them must have been chopped down long ago, for houses or furniture or firewood. Yet, in my gloved hand, I was holding onto a large leaf. Decades back, it had fallen out of the air. Sunk. Evidence now.

Q *The blood which you found on the claw portion of the hammer, –*

A *Yes, Sir.*

Q *– was that visible to the naked eye?*

A *Well, once you knew it was there, yes.*

I might as well put the kettle on.

A *It was just a small speck.*

Out the kitchen window, I see a tiny woman with shining white hair, down below in the grey light of morning. Mrs. Mackenzie. With her arms outstretched, she limps towards our brick building, before disappearing from view. I used to see her in the lobby getting mail. Since that phlebitis operation, she's hardly been visible.

> Q Well, did you examine it with your eye visually and see it before you examined it microscopically?
>
> A I could see – no, I do not recall whether I did or not.

Unprofessional.

The fridge shudders off. From somewhere, a plaintive cry.

I go back to my bedroom and see that Sunset has bellied under a mostly shut window. He is out on the narrow concrete ledge. Unable to turn on the narrow foothold, my cat is on the wrong side of the glass.

Not daring to breathe, I cross the carpet. If I slide the window up, Sunset might be bumped off or panicked into a suicidal leap.

Three stories below, Mrs. Mackenzie's arms are upraised to catch him. Waiting with bandaged legs. Her pink head almost bald when seen from up here. She could be killed if Sunset fell from this height.

What choice do I have? Wait and do nothing, and hope Sunset squirms back in. Take a chance, lift the window and grab at his falling fur?

Sunset looks at me expectantly through the glass.

Moves a front paw, tries to turn, and can't. Meows at me again, as I lift the sash slowly – ready to jerk it up instantly . . .

He twists away from my reaching hand, and thuds down, casually, on the bedroom carpet.

As Mrs. Mackenzie smiles up at me, I slam shut the window. Her upturned eyes, a blue that's close to green. I wave to her in thanks. So grateful, I wish I could lend her my young body for a week.

Craneflies in their Season

Struggling in the grass
or splayed against walls and fences,
they seem always somehow askew.
Even their flights in air
appear precarious
and all their moves seem
to be accidents.

Dead, they form windrows
of bent wires,
broken delicate parts
of some unexplained machine.
And the wind sweeps them
like evidence of an accident
out of sight.

• Pat Lowther

Thanksgiving Monday, October 13, 1975

I stare out through the slightly fogged windshield of the police car at our second-hand '68 Ford Fairlane, which needs a new transmission. It's parked sideways beneath high trees, fifty feet away, next to a large granite boulder by the picnic area.

I remember how less than an hour ago Mary and I got into an argument.

"Luke, don't look at me like that," she said.

"I'm not hungry."

"Then why did we drive all the way up here? I made cold chicken, and that potato salad you love."

I looked across at the face I knew better than my own and, with a brackish taste in my throat, told Mary I was sick of everything to do with food.

"OK Jennifer," Mary said, "it's raining on our picnic. Let's go back to the car and eat."

But Jennifer didn't want to.

Our daughter's head fell forward, long black hair flinging down to her waist. And she started to pick at a scab on her knee. Most of the summer brown gone from her straight legs. As she worked away at some nearly forgotten hurt, our two angry adult voices stopped. Mary couldn't take it anymore and said it would scar. Jennifer kept on, scraping at the hard, dark surface. I told her to let it fall off naturally. When she flicked a sharp fingernail under an edge, I wanted to slap her.

Had to turn my face away. Began walking towards the clear water, which was slipping past to the sea. I felt Mary's eyes right through my shirt, touching the skin on my back.

Now I'm sitting here, next to a man whose sharply creased pants have a broad yellow stripe down the side.

Jenny's hair no longer visible in the front passenger window of our Ford. She might be leaning towards Mary, or just slumped down. She used to have such happy lips. A stupid argument ...

"What is your place of employment?"

Startled, I glance across at the soft face of the Mountie. At his perfectly dented, wide-brimmed hat resting on the dash.

"The Terminal City Club."

"And your position there?"

"I am the head waiter." Who only wanted to relax, get back to nature for awhile, have a pleasant family outing. Forget about being polite. Instead, I sit upright and feel lost, while an RCMP officer takes down everything I say. The polished leather boot by the accelerator nearly the same brown as his eyes.

"Mr. Harding, how long have you been employed there?"

"Seventeen years." He looks barely that old.

The sudden squawk of his radio. The young Mountie leans forward to unhook the mouthpiece, "Corporal Cunningham here."

"This is Sergeant Pelletier, Squamish detachment."

"As a result of information I attended a body in Furry Creek."

"We'll be there in twelve minutes. Do not touch anything."

"The squad car is in the parking area next to the highway, south of the bridge at Furry Creek."

Terminal.

Beyond the sandy picnic beach, a rocky bank, slimey-green and slippery with life. Sweet-smelling cedars all around, and some alders whose coarse-toothed leaves stay green until they drop, and several tall firs. "Fir-y." Is that where the name comes from? Mary, her long nose always in a book, probably knows the origin. I'd remember if "Furry" was the name of one of those big-shots in a tight sports jacket who demands a special table at the Club, immediately. ("Right this way, Sir.")

"Mr. Harding, when did you first see it, exactly?"

"I don't know, I'm sorry. I don't wear a watch on my days off."

His mouth stays half-open, the tongue pressing against his short lower teeth. The upper ones curve out like a chipmunk's.

"In your estimation, how long did it take from the time of discovery to your phone call reporting it?"

"Five minutes, at most."

I glance at what he has written: "At 1415 hours on October 13th, 1975, the body of a woman was found lying face down in a body of water known as Furry Creek, located in the County of Vancouver, Province of British Columbia."

Near the mouth, where the railway bridge loomed, the creek level was so shallow that the water swept around the low, smooth stones on its way to the sea. To my left a large swipe of yellow in the sky where a big-leaf maple shimmered. Its bark mostly hidden by moss, but the leaves in a sudden flash of the sun looked like transparent gold.

To my right was a small clearing in high grasses, with the charred remains of a fire, where some hobo or hippies had taken shelter, or maybe a fisherman had tried to get warm. Or a family had picnicked.

Through the windshield I can see a dark-green sleeve moving. Jenny's arm waves at me from inside our car. A bit embarrassed, I make tiny, jerky movements of my hand from the wrist. She waves even harder – worried her grouchy father will be put in jail? I answer by throwing my whole arm and upper body around.

On the path I accidentally hit some rain off the drooping branches of a cedar tree, and wetted my hair and face. But I enjoyed the wakefulness of that dripping cold. Only wished I had brought my camera to photograph a river rock shaped like a lion's head. At my feet I found a huge maple leaf, which still burned bright except for brown edges on its top points.

Just before the shadow of the railway bridge, I stepping-stoned my way out to the middle of the river. Balancing on a rounded rock, I watched a water-striding insect walk on the surface.

"Mr. Harding, are you cold?"

"No, I'm fine." I am just a head waiter who wanted to be someone else.

Kneeling, I scooped up cold water in one hand and drank down to the map-lines of my cupped palm. The busy criss-crossings appeared accidental. Most of the creases disappearing over the edges of my hand.

"You're trembling. It could be delayed shock."

I squeeze my hands together, and see pink flood under my fingernails. The Mountie opens the car door, and I breathe in ozone, and drying kelp thrown up by the ocean, the lovely smell of cedar, the funk of ferns, deep mossy dampness, and all the wet, indiscriminate decay of growing things.

High above the horizontal line of the railway bridge, a gull glided towards me on a westerly, its feathers whiter than the starched linen napkins folded into fan shapes at the Club. I stared between the trestles, and saw how Furry Creek forked to the sea. Out in Howe Sound a tugboat and its log boom passed by. Before I noticed.

Corporal Cunningham holds out a white blanket with wide black stripes at the end. "A thing like this, you can't never tell how you'll react."

"Thanks." I feel childish but grateful as he drapes the heavy wool over my grown-up body.

"When the Sergeant gets here, he may need to ask you a few more questions."

35

His baby face blushed at what I had pointed to.

I had only wanted a happy Thanksgiving holiday with my family, near the forest, next to a flowing river. All at once in the water ahead of me, a large thing, fish-belly white. The nightmare outside of my head.

"The other squad car should be here soon."

"OK."

We've been arguing a lot lately. Noisy vibrating sounds coming out of my throat, shouting in a way I don't dare at the Club when a busboy screws up.

"Why didn't you pick up my other suit? You don't care if I bring a paycheque home?" Hammering Mary with my frustrations.

"Luke, please. Jennifer had a toothache. I took her to the dentist, where we had to wait more than an hour and a half for an opening . . . "

Felt like an idiot and an ogre when Jenny opened her mouth to show me the new filling. I smiled stupidly at the light-grey speck of amalgam. Didn't say I was sorry.

A faraway siren.

Mary used to let her body relax its weight against me like I was a tree trunk. That first time at pink dusk, and the freighters out in the bay had their lights winking on, and the sand in my socks didn't matter.

That picture I took of her in Stanley Park, leaning against a big cedar tree. She was reaching back with both arms to feel at the bark, which was the same colour as her hair, blowing red-brown across her face.

When we were new together. Mary taught me about the rounded bodies of trees. The woven strips of cedar bark, the grey-green smoothness on alder, the scab-like plates for pine, the creamy-white and peelable sheets covering birch, the scales on spruce, the deep ridges of old Douglas Fir trees, and hemlock with patches like human skin cells.

The flashing light races towards us.

I'd just like to be home with my three-lobed family. Melting a bar of European chocolate, heating up a pond of milk, scalding it until the steam starts to rise, then blending the two together before heaping in spoonfuls of brown sugar. Taking down from the hooks everyone's favourite mugs.

Corporal Cunningham steps outside smartly, and tilts down the brim of his Mountie hat: a straight line across his forehead.

The other dark blue car brakes sharply, rocks up and down. Two Mounties get out, slam doors, and smack their boots against the highway. One holds a walkie-talkie, the other, a camera in a black case slung over his shoulder.

"Corporal, where is it?"

"Down over there, Sir."

Will I have to go back down there with them? Half-tripping on the blanket, I climb out of the police car into a gentle rain that has just begun.

"This is Mr. Harding, the person who discovered the body."

"And what time was that?"

"I don't have a watch."

"You called from the Gulf station?"

"It was just a few minutes before that."

"The call came in at 1420 hours."

"Can I see my family now?"

"Soon. Mr. Harding, when you first saw the body, what position was it in?"

"Well, it was lying face-down, and its head was jammed under a log."

"Did you touch or in any way move the body?"

"No, Sir." I just let go of a broad maple leaf, and watched as it turned over once in the wind before floating downstream, its pale underside up. Saw it drift by her legs, which were like a frog's at rest.

"Mr. Harding, that's all we need at present."

Jenny waves tiredly at me. Her teenage face still a bit tanned from a summer of swimming. I can still remember her tadpole body wriggling fast through the water . . .

"You are free to go."

Mary has stepped out of the far side of our car. Her bare arm, lying on the wet metal roof, turns its open hand this way. As I walk towards her, I see dozens of bright droplets clinging to her cedar hair.

Spitball

His hands flicker
brown on the white
costume, the green arena;
a shuttling dance,
all stations touched
Earth, thighs,
heart, the head
covering, the mouth
also moves, chewing
herbs and invocations.
The hands weave wind,
the watchers' tension,
prayers, sweat
from the forehead,
and unseen in the swift
dazzle of motion
the magic spittle
points the ball.

• Pat Lowther

Wednesday evening, October 15, 1975

Why wouldn't Ron tell me on the phone?

I crumple up my damp cotton shirt, throw it across the bed, and it catches on the spike of the standing lamp. Even my bra is wet from the downpour.

There's a roar from the TV. I rush back into the living room to see Ken Griffey standing on second base. And Johnny Bench is up next. On the mound, Luis Tiant, the chunky right-hander with the Fu Manchu moustache, looks sad and tired, and it's only the bottom of the first inning. The rain is beating hard against the window. A wet fall, winter, and spring to get through before softball season can begin again. I hate to get in a shower, even if the water's hot. But I need to rinse the chemical fumes out of my hair. When this World Series ends, there will only be lactic phenol memories of summer.

I am heading for the bathroom when there's another roar from the fans at Riverfront Stadium in

Cincinnati. Johnny Bench hustles into second base: another double. Already Boston is down 2-0 to the Big Red Machine. I should just admit I'm a woman living alone, and move the TV into the bedroom.

What is his big news?

Today's paper says "Liz and Dick remarried."

> CHOBE, Botswana (AP) – Miss Taylor, 43, and Burton, 49, were reconciled in Switzerland in August after 14 months of divorce. They were married first in 1964 – she for the fifth time and he for the second – after a romance that began when they were co-starring in the movie Cleopatra in Rome.

He's the one who suggested we give each other "some space."

> Miss Taylor wore a green dress edged with lace and decorated with guinea-fowl feathers. The bridegroom was in a red shirt, open at the neck, white slacks, red socks and white shoes.

Don't be a romantic fool, Olga.

> . . . drank champagne toasts on a river bank in Botswana while two hippos looked on.

Could be here any moment. As I push the shower curtain aside, the phone rings. Is he cancelling me again? In the mirror, this head of mine always looks too big: like a newborn's. The big baby my parents didn't want.

Reluctantly, I pull my dressing gown on, and go to the bedside phone. "Hello."

"Olga, you sound underwater."

"Hi, Emily. I was about to step into the shower, though I'm already drenched. My umbrella blew inside out, then I dumped the rain it had collected on top of my head."

"That's too bad, Olga. But listen, we have to go see the Donnelly trilogy at Simon Fraser. It's by James Reaney, and has this simultaneity thing. A couple of actors dramatize an event while at the same time miming where the incident began, and they also show the audience what's going to happen next."

"Fine, Emily. Can you get the tickets? I've got to run. Which night?"

"The play lasts for *three* nights."

"What if I have a date?"

"Olga, have you got a new man in your life?"

Just the same funny little man I met a few years ago, at the nursery. "Can I let you know tomorrow?"

"OK. Bye, you rudesby."

"Bye, Emily."

I glance in at the game. Luis Tiant, the man with a million motions, is struggling out there, throwing too many fast balls. Still 2-0. Ron's herky-jerky motions towards commitment have tantalized me far too long. He probably had to work outside in the rain, transplanting shrubs and trees. His breaking ball is doing nothing, moving nowhere, and we're already down 2-1 in the series.

GUN DUELS RAGE IN BEIRUT

POT THERAPY URGED

Tiant rolls off the mound towards the dugout, having survived the first inning. I've got to get into that shower.

> WEATHER: Cloudy with showers Thursday, turning to steady rain in the evening.

I live inside a rain forest in a body that is mainly water.

The fingers of the deceased woman were so wrinkled and parchment-like, we had to cut them off at the first joint. In an advanced state of decomposition.

> WOMAN'S BODY FOUND
> Vancouver police are assisting in the identification of a woman's body found Monday in the Squamish area. Police Inspector S. A. Ziola said detectives went to Squamish shortly after the badly decomposed body was found "to have a look." The woman had probably been dead "three to four weeks" and identification was not immediately possible, he said. Detectives said a man found the naked body partially submerged in Furry Creek in the Britannia Beach area.

The unstoppable moisture of this world. I feel nearly as water-logged as her.

I placed each of her cut-off fingers in a vial, soaked them in lactic phenol solution to make them pliable, but still had to tie them off and insert a hypodermic needle into the bulbous part to make them round enough to dust with fingerprint powder. And even then I couldn't get a clear print when I rolled the finger ends onto the acetate lifter. Ironic, I've grown up to identify strangers when I've never been able to find out who my parents were. Are? An adopted child, I'll never, knowingly, see a face related to my own.

Boston can't hit their left-hander, Fred Norman. Got to get a move on.

I shrug off my robe, and it feels like the shower has, by a weird kind of osmosis, reached my skin even before I've turned on a tap. As the water heats up, something loosens in my back, and inside my tangled brain. Maybe Tiant has settled down now. He's certainly pitching with heart.

I could wear the bright orange top with black pants. Or maybe my peasant blouse with the green skirt, and new stockings? And guinea fowl feathers! Why have I ended up wearing orange plastic gloves, and holding a soft, bony finger end? Jamming down hard to press the tip flat, but still couldn't get anything usable for I.D.

I twist shut the shower and lunge for a towel. A buzzer? With water in my ears, I listen, but hear nothing more. I rub at my face and hair, and dry the bottom of my feet on the bath mat.

That cellophane and cardboard package contains stockings that are supposed to give my legs a smooth, silky look. Kayser, the colour: Stormcloud.

I wonder what inning we're in now. It's not exactly a surprise Boston's losing, given that the Big Red Machine has a 67-17 home record this year. Rose,

44

Griffey, Morgan, Bench, Perez, and someone like George Foster hitting sixth. Maybe I'll check on the score before I get dressed.

The buzzer, definitely. I throw on my orange top, and pull up my black pants. My hair stuck to my face. I kick on the black shoes lying on their sides, and stride to the door without my new stormcloud stockings.

Ron, who holds flowering plants in one hand, looks up at me like a drowned leprechaun.

"Come in, come in."

He steps neatly out of a gumboot by scrunching down one rubber toe on top of the other. This man is not Richard Burton with red socks and white shoes.

But I breathe in sweet-smelling clusters of orange-centred blooms. "Narcissus?"

"Tazettas, Babe. I kept the bulbs cool and dark for three months, so they are fooled into thinking they've been through winter."

Ron tries to hand me the miniature flowers while I'm helping him take off his coat. I tug, but his arm won't come out; it's as though he's roped in. Finally, the soaked sleeve slips free, and his heavy coat drops to the floor. A red tomato rolls across the linoleum as we stand beside each other, laughing.

"Babe, I didn't think you wanted to go out in the rain again, so I brought some grub over." Like a magician, he pulls out of his shirt pocket a sprig of rosemary, a couple of fresh bay leaves, and snips of variegated thyme. With a half-baked grin, Ron reaches into the back pocket of his pants, and pulls out a head of garlic.

45

"Bravo."

I tilt down my big head as he comes up at me, with an urgent kiss. Unprepared for his lips pressing into mine this much, this soon, I almost drop the flowers. I have to ask myself, again, why a woman would leave this man.

"I love their scent, Ron. Thank you. I'll hang your coat in the bathroom."

"Who's winning the ball game?"

"Cincinnati." But it looks as though Boston is scoring some runs right now. A triple by Dwight Evans! "2-2. You've brought the Red Sox good luck." I breathe in the rich fragrance of the tiny flowers, then set their container on the glass table next to the TV.

His curled hand removes five more Italian tomatoes from his coat pocket, and sets them on the arborite counter.

"I'll be back in a moment. Tell me what's happening."

"A guy just belted a double," he shouts.

"You mean it's 3-2 for Boston?"

"I guess so, Babe." His agile hands are peeling a garlic bud.

"Here's a towel for your wet hair. Look, Cincinnati just booted the ball. The Big Red Machine is falling apart! 4-2 Boston." I open the fridge. "Do you want a beer?"

"Sure. Don't bother with a glass. I'm not one of those high-rent type of guys."

A roofing contractor who quit his business, to work in a garden nursery. "I'll put on some water to boil.

Look, Yastrzemski hit a single. We're leading 5-2. What a turn-around."

He nods, staring at the empty shelf above the cans, one of his hands holding on to the open cupboard door.

"Ron, what's your news?"

"Ginger is getting hitched again."

What do I care about his ex-wife? I switch off the TV.

"She tells me he's some big-shot at MacBlo."

He doesn't look at me, just down at the tomato he's rinsing, rolling it over and over in his strong hand.

"This new guy wants to adopt Shannon."

And?

He opens a drawer and pulls out a sharp knife, starts to chop, chop.

"I need to ask you something serious, Babe."

No sheen of a wedding ring in sight. But Ron might pull one out of his ear as the final magic trick of the evening. "Yes."

"Do you know how these things work?"

"What?"

"It would save me child support payments, big-time – I pay a whack of them each month. But no way am I going to sign away my own flesh and blood."

COMATOSE WOMAN 'HAS A CHANCE' The court-appointed guardian for Karen Anne Quinlan says the 21-year-old comatose. . . .

No way.

The girl's parents, Mr. and Mrs.

Joseph Quinlan, are seeking a court order to direct doctors to remove their daughter from the respirator. They contend. . . .

"I know I should get a lawyer, but where do I find the coin?"

Daniel Coburn said Miss Quinlan's condition may not be irreversible, as her adoptive parents have alleged. Coburn, a lawyer, states in his brief that "in all probability, Karen can survive without the use of the respirator." But he warned that disconnecting the machine could hasten her death.

I look up from the newspaper, then across to the stove. Hundreds of tiny bubbles form and break in the pot.

"Olga?"

"I'm sure your consent would be needed."

His face glows in gratefulness, as though I've just rescued Shannon from the darkest dungeon. Ron sets down his can of beer and squeezes me, his scratchy face against my chest for a moment.

"Anything interesting in the paper today?"

Liz and Dick got remarried. "Not really. The usual stuff. Strikes, wars, corpses, kidnapping." It's nice to have a man in my kitchen sautéing garlic in olive oil.

Ron dices a tomato quickly and precisely, then dumps the segments into the pan. With his shirt open at the neck, I can see that every second hair is white.

I toss some salt into the big pot of boiling water, and the "poof" startles me as usual. His darting eyes watch while I stir in a big handful of noodles.

"Olga." He scrunches up a tiny yellow and green leaf, holds it under my nose and tickles my nostrils. "Lemon thyme."

I breathe in its citrus scent. "Yes." His curved fingernails pull backwards on a thin brown stem, and the yellow-green stars fall down on the wooden board.

"I'm thinking about going out on a limb."

I stop opening the tin of clams, and listen.

"I want to start up a landscaping business."

Out on a limb. I try to change my laughter into words: "You'd be good at it."

"Thanks, but my last business went belly-up."

I can think of nothing to say. "Your heart would be in it this time." People can always find more words.

"You know, Babe, I've been thinking … when things get quiet after the Christmas sales, the nursery lays off its staff, so maybe in January we could hightail it to some place warm, like Mexico."

Why does this guy believe I'll keep fitting my life into his schedule? I am suddenly floating, face-down, in the liquid tomato flavours of my own kitchen.

I turn away and click on the TV. Tiant in a jam again, but still out there. I watch him throw two balls in a row.

"Babe, did I say something wrong?"

"I'm just checking the score." I turn off the TV. "Ron, I'm not waiting around to fill your vacant slots."

"Olga, I didn't mean . . . I just tripped over my tongue. I love you."

His ordinary words sound tentative, almost new.

As I dump the clams into the sauce, Ron stirs them with a wooden spoon, then hugs me, and my ignorant body feels grateful. I feel a flush of desire colour my face and throat. Itchy and alive, my nerve endings gorge with blood. Unhappy when he lets go, and scampers away to the bathroom.

Outside, only black rain. But by the TV's grey screen, bright flowers grow like it's springtime. Ron's zest is dangerous. I could easily risk too much, needing to forget the dead stretched out every day in front of me.

I turn the set back on: Tiant *still* on the mound. An excellent sign, but he's obviously labouring. He throws a ball to Pete Rose, with a runner on second. Bottom of the ninth, and Boston leading 5-4. There is a relaxed excitement to watching men's bodies move for reasons that are clear and measurable (and trivial). Another ball. He's being too careful. Fisk's throw back to his pitcher has just that little extra juice on it, saying to Luis, I know you're tired, you've been out there a long time, but concentrate now: we can win this thing. Another ball, and Rose is sprinting to first base with what could be the winning run. The Cincinnati fans are screaming with Griffey at the plate. Again this year, it looks as though no World Series champagne will be drunk by Boston.

I set out another can of beer for Ron, then lift the sagging noodles onto two large plates as Tiant pitches.

Griffey connects, rocketing the ball deep to centre field beyond Lynn – who races back to make a *stunning* over-the-head catch. The crowd shuts up and I'm yelling.

Ron runs back into my living room, and I hug him.

Luis rotates the ball in his right hand, feeling for the red stitches. The Red Sox need only one more out, but Joe Morgan is up. Ron kisses my cheekbone. The pitch, and it's an infield pop-up to Yastrzemski. Don't drop it. Yes! I embrace Ron even tighter as teammates swarm Luis, whose fist is raised in victory. The series now all tied up.

"Babe, you give me a hard-on."

I glance down: a miniature baseball bat shape.

Maybe tonight his magic spit will give me a new life. A face like my own.

Octopus

The octopus is beautifully
functional as an umbrella;
at rest a bag of rucked skin
sags like an empty scrotum
his jelled eyes sad and bored

but taking flight: look
how lovely purposeful
in every part:
the jet vent smooth
as modern plumbing
the webbed pinwheels of tentacles
moving in perfect accord
like a machine dreamed
by Leonardo

• Pat Lowther

Wednesday afternoon, October 15, 1975

My son's breath is visible on the cool glass. A fold of skin covers the gills of the *Octopus vulgaris,* a large predator that typically reproduces once and dies.

"It's not going to move, Dad."

"Sometimes, Billy, you have to be persistent to see things. When they jet-propel themselves around, they eject water from their mantle violently, and steer by turning their siphon."

"It's asleep."

Brenda's protrusive orbital bones define his face. ("You just lie there, expecting me to turn you on.") Sometimes I'd rather just go into a hair salon where an attractive young woman hangs up your coat, cradles your occipital lobe in gentle hands, eases your head onto the lip of the sink with a fluffy white towel, and sprays you with needles of wet heat as her strong fingers massage herbal shampoo into your sliding scalp . . .

"It looks dead."

"Billy, a few decades ago the corpse of a giant squid drifted up onto a beach in New Zealand. Each eye measured 40 centimetres across. That's bigger than any other creature's. As wide as your chest." I squeeze his rib-cage between my curving index fingers like callipers, and he jumps away, embarrassed.

"It could just be pretending, you know. An octopus is a very bright creature, Billy. Only a few years ago, right here at the Vancouver Aquarium, rare tropical fish started disappearing and no one could figure out how. They suspected vandalism, so they set up a video camera, and waited. It showed an octopus, maybe this very guy, waiting until nighttime when no one was around, squeezing itself out of a narrow air shaft, sliding down a glass wall, sliming its way across the floor, and then climbing into the tropical fish tank for a midnight snack. And before the staff arrived for work the next morning, it had sneaked back."

"Can we go see *Jaws* again?"

"Do you mean go visit the shark tank, and watch it swim around, endlessly?"

"Nah, you know, the *movie*."

He hammers at the aquarium glass with his small fist.

Still the image-forming eye doesn't open. "It's hard to believe these smart, eight-legged things evolved from clams that managed to trap gas inside their shells and float."

"Dad, school's over for today, OK?"

I'm supposed to be at work still, completing an autopsy on that diver who drowned in a training pool with a full tank of air on his back. For an unknown reason, his face mask was off, and a working air regulator wasn't in his mouth. And that woman who was pulled from a river, whose fingertips Olga sliced off in hopes of establishing an I.D. What a baseball nut. She wanted to talk to me, a Brit, about the World Series. I couldn't make her shut her gob about the Reds and the Red Sox, which are ironic names for American teams, given their dread of Commies. My examination of the fractured skull indicated some fairly heavy-edged instrument.

Billy kicks up his small, dark-blue running shoe, missing the glass. He steps on a dirty-white lace that's dangling, stumbles a bit, then flings an elbow at the wall, before he runs off, wincing.

Now the octopus opens an eye. Observing me. Like we vertebrates, its brain can distinguish among classes of objects imaged on its retina. Is he angry at me?

When I came home at noon to fetch my pills, some fellow was all over Brenda like an octopus.

A double row of suckers on the inert tentacles, but one of those resting tentacles is used as a large penis to shove bags of spermatozoa into the cavity of the female's underside. Vulgar.

The image-forming eye shuts.

Brenda and I met at the cinema. Our shared delight partly derived from watching life being enacted, and figuring it out together with a bag of popcorn: Fellini, Antonioni, Bergman, Kurosawa, Ozu, Ray, Wajda, Forman, Godard, Truffaut. Billy is now acting like the unhappy kid in *The 400 Blows*, Jean-Pierre Léaud.

He waits for me by the shark tank, watching the white belly and the double rows of teeth turn sideways to the glass in silent passing.

"Come on, Billy. I'll buy you a coke and a packet of crisps."

"A bag of potato chips, Dad."

I'm still out of linguistic place in *British* Columbia. And, really, I should not be eating junk food in the late afternoon. "Two cokes, please." When Father told me that one day I would become a doctor too, and as fat as he, I thought he must be jesting. All this flesh I didn't want. Back then, tearing around the rugby pitch, tackling the fastest wingers … "And these bags of crisps."

Billy takes his stuff to the table without waiting for me to pay, and bites at the corner of the shiny aluminium, ripping it wide open. Before I even sit down, he is crunching away.

I tear open my packet and reach in, craving salt. Biting through the shell-like resistance, I munch along with my son. I swallow the salty paste in my mouth and try to speak to him about her: "When your mother and I first met, we would go to the pictures every Friday. Brenda and I would see movies from all over the world: France, Italy, Japan, Poland, Czechoslovakia, Sweden. We talked and laughed and talked about them sometimes past midnight." No response. I concentrate on eating.

When my mother wrote from Bristol asking William what he would like for a Christmas present, he scrawled on the bottom of my letter, "Money for a gitar." Nearly twelve, he's been born into a generation of near-illiterates who can't even spell their favourite object. I feel in my pocket for the paperback dictionary that I bought yesterday, before the incident. Webster's, not the Oxford, because William has become a North American in British Columbia. "I picked this up for you, sort of an early birthday gift."

He bends his slender neck sideways, looks at me quizzically, then takes the paperback from my greasy fingers. His little thumb flicks at the pages, fluttering their edges. Now he spins through them so that only the right-hand margins are visible. It's too fast to read any words anyway, since one page blurs into the next. William sets the paperback aside, next to his torn empty foil.

I pull the dictionary closer, and open it to the beginning of the alphabet. "Here, let me show you something, Billy." Rapidly, I sketch a man high up in the right-hand margin, another stick-man on the next page, a third on the following page, another, and another – getting faster – until this black-inked figure with arms and legs in slightly altered positions appears on the top right-hand corner of a dozen consecutive pages. I twist the book on the table towards Billy, and with my large thumb flip through those pages. Jerkily, the inky man begins to run, almost like a rugby player.

Billy smiles. He scratches at his springy hair, then grabs the pen out of my hand. He makes some kind of design at the bottom right of the first page of his new dictionary. A biggish circle with triangle points inside, and now a horizontal figure.

"It's a trick of the human eye that makes moving pictures possible, Billy. We see a brief after-image, when, in fact, there is nothing except a blank celluloid strip before the sprockets of the projector drag down the next picture. It's called 'the persistence of vision.'"

On page after page of the dictionary, he draws the same female body with arms and legs flung out in different positions.

About to come into puberty, I guess. "Billy, you might be interested in an optical trick used in early movies, called the Schüfftan process. It let you put in any background you wanted for an action. Fritz Lang used this technique for *Metropolis*." He's too busy with my pen to listen, but you never know. "First, you'd build the miniature set, then scrape the silver off the middle of a mirror face, which would be mounted in front of the camera lens at a 45-degree angle. Then you could shoot actors through the scraped-off part of the mirror as they moved around, and because the made-up scenery would be reflected in the silver surface, it would look as if they were moving in the real world." In live action, like Brenda and myself.

His head bent to his task, but now hurrying his lines too much as they are starting to sprawl together. The skull's ball-like structure is like that of an octopus.

In my packet only broken bits of crisps left.

"Billy, do you want to stay with me for awhile and get some dinner? We could eat at Simpatico's, where you might have a pizza." Only the silence of his concentration. It would be fitting for me to order the calamari. The octet rule in chemistry. For most atoms the number of electrons needed to fill the outermost ring is eight, and joining others they tend towards that maximum number, balancing the positive and negative charges.

He places the pen on the table between us. Without looking up at me, Billy flicks the pages. A menacing, sharp-toothed jaw opens and closes as a shark chases a swimmer, then bites off her leg. He closes the dictionary. Raising his eyes, he asks, "Why did you hit Mom?"

His question, a sudden blow.

Jealousy, rage, hurt, betrayal of a happy life together. It's amusing – even hilarious – to sit in the cinema and watch a character being cuckolded, a character on whom the audience can't spare its emotion. His anger makes him even funnier, but to walk into your own bedroom and see your slippers lined with fake fur waiting there in the corner as some long-armed stranger slimes into his jeans and sneaks his John Lennon glasses back onto a sharp nose … Your wife has a sheet over her breasts and a face like a shiny red apple. I can't explain. "Billy, I'm sorry."

A contusion around Brenda's left orbital bone. Muffiekins my nickname for her. Mine used to be Plum: the bruise almost the same colour.

Our son picks up the dictionary, his thumb poised to flutter the pages again, but he merely scratches at the paper edges with his thumbnail. Then he puts the book down without flipping any pages, looks at me cautiously.

Did fear make him jump, earlier, at my caliper touch?

"Simpatico's, then?"

"Nah, I'd better go home," Billy says.

from **Chacabuco, the Pit**

Notice first the magnificent sunset,
the stars, the clouds of Magellan.
Note that here as in all human places
prayer has been uttered.

Watch until morning
burns the sky white.
Wooden shacks persevere
in the dry air,
their corners banked with dust;
a grid of streets prints
an ominous white shadow
on your eyelids;
it leads
to the pit.

A huge, gouged cavity
flickering like a bad film,
the whole scene twitching
on and off
in and out of existence:
is God blinking? are you
shuttering your eyes, tourista?

• Pat Lowther

Thursday evening, October 16, 1975

I first *spoke* to Pablo three weeks ago. When the newspapers were full of stories about an eight-year-old boy wandering barefoot by Kitsilano Beach, with greenish bruises on each temple. His name was Mark. Skin and bones and a distended stomach. Mark had apparently never been to school in his life, and had rarely been let outside. Later, the VGH reported he was "in satisfactory condition," so the media forgot him.

I first *saw* Pablo (I now realize) around the second anniversary of the coup. Startled by his wistful, milk-chocolate eyes staring out from a basement window at my feet clicking past on the sidewalk. Somehow I felt no fear at his watching.

I first *heard* of Pablo from Mrs. Chesnick a few months before that. When she mentioned renting out her basement room to a grad student in geography. Though she didn't know what country he was from.

Chile like a long, torn-off strip of paper, its lower end curling in the air.

He has no phone, so I try to imagine him, at this moment, moving in the geography of a Vancouver basement room. Which perhaps is narrow like his homeland? Pablo stoops under heating pipes as he circumnavigates a hot round furnace. I imagine him stepping through oily dust on his way to a varnished, rickety table that is his desk. A bright bulb, in a goose-necked lamp? Only a block away, I imagine love.

Pablo, a kind of orphan. Which, at my age, makes me halfway between a lover and a mother. Pablito. My baby? I must remember not to call him by the diminutive.

I first spoke to Pablo three weeks ago in the drizzling rain. His long back against the wooden bus stop, his arms squeezing an open newspaper tight to his chest. He was crying.

I must have smiled or nodded, or looked sad, or, more Canadianly, embarrassed. This tall, black-haired young man spread his arms out, and showed me a large photo of a freighter that had been battered on the rocks, off the coast of Chile. The ship pointed brokenly in two different directions. Puckering and soggy, the picture of the *Northern Breeze* was tearing in his hands as Pablo continued to weep on the rain-wet newsprint. I stood there falling in love with a man unashamed by his tears.

Outside right now, this heavy, flooding rain sounds like the world is ending.

On our second bus ride together, he told me he was interested in the ways man-made structures modify coastlines.

I must have blushed when Pablo used the word "groin." A barrier that projects directly seaward from the shore, he told me, with a quick smile. Built to trap a portion of the littoral drift, groins can add to an existing upstream beach that otherwise might be eroded, but can starve the downdrift side of sand. A boat-launching ramp can unintentionally erode a neighbour's property. I got the drift of what he meant while my head drifted off into romance. Washed away.

Like past loves?

Like a giddy school girl, I have to fight this foolish urge to run out into this amazing downpour and race the block and a half to Pablo's low window, which is half-underground. Rap on the smeary glass until he lets me in – hugs me in those long arms – warms my slippery skin. Love must be an erosion of the brain.

Erosion, what my father fears about inflation. Day by day, his little life-savings become worthless.

Another briefing tomorrow morning on the wage and price controls legislation, which Trudeau in an expensive suit stepped out of a limousine to announce. The Anti-inflation Review Board he's created is definitely unfair to thousands of workers on the verge of concluding new agreements. Ottawa has been bargaining in bad faith. But what about people like Dad, who are suffering? It's a trade-off.

Sometimes it's hard to know whether he's awake or asleep. I fear one day I'll find him sitting in front of a TV with chirpy voices and shining faces, not breathing.

Tonight the Minister's Assistant wants me to eyeball a long list of consumer price hikes, so Phyllis

Young will be prepped for reporters. I should check on Dad. Last week at Safeway, after lifting his handful of groceries onto the counter one item at a time, he flinched every time the check-out woman punched in the new price.

I call from the hallway: "Dad?"

"In here, Cath." His yellow-brown eyes appear owlish behind round tortoise-shell frames.

"Have you seen a blue pen?"

His beaky head swivels away from the doorway to the TV and back to me. "No."

"I must've left it in the kitchen."

"The rain is making a great din."

"Yes, I hope our roof doesn't leak."

"It won't, princess. It's only six years old."

"Enjoy your programme."

"I'm just waiting for the news."

"OK. Maybe I'll join you later. I have some work to do first."

He never seemed to mind the chauffeur's cap that designated him a servant to the rich. His funhouse face always grinned in the sharp fins of the black Caddie he had just polished. Forever cleaning and adjusting the mirrors of some kind of big car. I remember once how his blue cap disappeared into the sun reflecting off the painted hood of a blue Rolls, and how he beamed like the proud owner. He never seemed to feel my rage and confused shame. Dad wouldn't be made miserable by life's lottery. Even now, he can't get angry at a thing like inflation.

Too astounded to be upset when I joined the NDP.

Or when I broke up with my boyfriends, who assumed my cheerful subservience.

Pablo not the same? We haven't even kissed yet. Our only "date" a stroll near Wreck Beach, between the war towers, checking the "average recession rate" of the cliffs. He expects that the splendid anthropology museum above, with all its glass and concrete, will come tumbling down. He's equally convinced that the CIA used inflation to bring down the Allende government.

We talked about everything. The Northern Breeze, I should be called.

("A spit is what, Pablo?"

"I have to teach you English? Sometimes it is called a 'hook.'")

Actually, we talked mostly about his studies, in oceanography.

("It used to be believed that detached breakwaters constructed parallel to the coast, like the one at Santa Monica, would allow free littoral drift and avoid sediment build-up. However, it turns out, they block the local waves that carry the sand along the shore evenly. As a consequence, in the shadow zone behind the breakwater, a spit grows out from the beach that will eventually reach it. A natural barrier such as Percé Rock in Québec, or Frank Island just south of Chesterman Beach on Vancouver Island, has the same effect. It impedes the along-shore transport of beach material, so that a sandy spit forms in the lee, which, in time, becomes a *tombolo*."

"A *tombolo*?"

"A spit that reaches so far out that the island becomes joined to the coastline. In Italy, there are many."

"So then you can walk from the shore all the way out to what used to be an island?"

"At low tide. *Si*.")

Pablo sort of invited me to go away next weekend with him in a friend's car, to the Pacific Rim National Park, to look at Frank Island, observe how a spit turns into a *tombolo*. ("If it interests you, Cathy.") *Si*. It's been years since I've felt the power of the Pacific coming all the way from Japan.

In this pounding rainstorm Pablo must be sick with worry about the battering of his cliffs by high waves. But the huge wind, I think, is coming from the east, and Pablo said it was the northwest storms that do the most damage. It's like he feels responsible for literally saving the earth.

Beware of Latin American guys, Emily warns. They can be very, very handsome, but their *machismo* comes from a truly ugly, racist past, she says. Too negative a slant because her boyfriend from Argentina left her? Conquistadores. No different in Canada. Pablito, a man who cries for his country and for his older brother, Miguel, executed by the junta.

Fell in love with his English sea words tongued by a Spanish mouth: "beach cusps," "navigable channels," "jetties," "groin." But that Italian word, *tombolo*. It sounds both funny and ominous: a comic tumble or a small tomb?

Every morning, Dad – who's been up for at least an hour – waits for me at the kitchen table so he has company while he chews on his cold toast and marmalade, and sips at watery tea. I'm usually running around with an unzipped purse slung over my shoulder, a cup sloshing coffee, a hand shoving half-read reports back into a jammed briefcase.

With an election coming up soon, there will be a Noah's Flood of meetings. I'd love to disappear to a sunny place like Santa Monica or Italy where ...

Crash! I'd better see what he's done now.

In the bathroom, he sways over the sink, staring down. Pajamas hang from his sharp shoulders. Hooked fingers hold a jagged drinking glass upside down. He does not know what to do next.

"Here, let me take that."

"I'm sorry, Cath."

"Don't worry. You're not cut?"

The hand with its thin gold band wavers in the air. Its pale palm only inches from his face. Slowly, he rotates his hand: no blood on the wrinkly, brown-speckled skin. He now catches sight of a gaunt, grey-stubbled man in the mirror. In polite wonderment, Dad gazes at himself.

I lift the wet, transparent shards out of the sink, which is dirty with hardened toothpaste. They drop to the bottom of the jagged drinking glass with soft clinks. A few smaller pieces must have gone down the drain.

I pat Dad on his shoulder before carrying the fragments inside the broken glass to the kitchen. To be thrown out.

Like Salvador Allende, the doctor who founded the Chilean Socialist Party. Both Pablo and Miguel supported him, the first freely elected Marxist leader in the Western Hemisphere, if not the world. During the bloody military coup two years ago, Allende died, allegedly by his own hand. But his wife said he was murdered on General Augusto Pinochet's orders for nationalizing the copper mines and pushing for huge land reforms. And the Nobel prize-winning poet, Pablo Neruda, ended up dead too in that first week of the coup, supposedly of a heart attack. A month later, in the Desert of Atacama, Miguel.

Lanky like his country, Pablito comes to this rainy northern English place that is still on the Pacific. Starts work on an elaborate project to stop the eroding. His first summer here, Pablo helps design and build a series of groins and berms. A sophisticated structure that's filled with sand and cobble rocks, stretching nearly a mile along the beach. Then, in February, fierce storm-generated waves tear away at the base, and thousands of tons of sand wash away into the Straight of Georgia. Another man-made scheme fails. The grey-brown cliffs below UBC continue to erode, at an average recession rate of six inches a year. Weathering.

Poor Pablito. But maybe he and his brother came from a rich family who had a chauffeur?

There's the phone. It's late.

"Hello."

"Cath, it's Emily."

"Hi."

"I have some bad, bad news."

The space inside my skull suddenly grown large. Now contracts down to something very tiny.

"I'm sorry to have to tell you this. Are you sitting down, Cath?"

The whole room breathes in and out.

"It's about Pat Lowther."

"Oh no." A stranger is being told this news.

"I'm afraid she's ..."

"No." I'm not here, listening to the blood beat in my forehead. Beat.

"They identified her."

"Oh, Em." My body shuddering with the room.

"They found her body near Britannia Beach."

And I've slumped to the floor. "I used to talk to her almost every day. When she was Phyllis Young's secretary."

"Cath, apparently she was murdered."

Only happens in movies, or on TV. "Why? Who?" Pat?

"I don't know. They're arranging a memorial service for next Friday evening. At the Unitarian Church on West 49th."

"Two young daughters, Em."

"It's too, too sad."

"So young." All wrong. "Too unimaginable."

"Ever since Pat didn't show up for her poetry reading at the Ironworkers Hall, somehow I *knew* something was wrong. But, Cath, can I phone you back in a few minutes to talk some more? There's another call I should make before it gets too late."

"Of course. Thanks, Emily."

"Bye. Take care."

"You too. Bye."

Hot, salty water floods down my cheeks. Both these women like half-sisters. One suddenly gone. No, killed.

Startled by a hand softly patting at my hair. Dad must have come into the kitchen while I was on the phone.

"It'll be OK, princess."

No. For Pat, the end of the world, and all our days worth less.

from **To Capture Proteus**

In water
all shapes are separate
as my limbs are apart from me
moving like other swimmers

• Pat Lowther

Monday early evening, October 20, 1975

All the cupboard doors flung open.

"Alex, have you seen a box of rice?"

"Marilyn, I just got home from the crime site. And before that I was working on Mayne Island for three days. Give me a break."

"So you haven't seen a box of Uncle Ben's converted rice? I'm sure I bought one last week."

"Maybe we should move to a gulf island when the twins grow up a bit more. I love the way the arbutus trees there lean out to sea, and their limbs twist unpredictably. They never grow straight up, and they shed their bark continuously. Right now they have these clusters of bright orange berries that are on their way to becoming a dark red."

"Potatoes with chicken OK for dinner?"

"Fine. Where are the kids?"

Marilyn flicks on the stove, and holds a wrist out at me. "Lisa's in her room. She was at her friend Anne's

73

wedding on Saturday. Your daughter came home really excited, her cheeks flushed with champagne. She must have talked to me for an hour afterwards."

"Maybe she borrowed your box of rice to throw at the bride and groom?"

Marilyn taps shut the cupboard doors. "He's a milkman, with three kids, Lisa told me. His wife got killed a year and a half ago in a car accident on the Trans-Canada Highway. Driving back from Winnipeg where her father was dying of cancer. It's all very romantic for Lisa. Anne's just turned sixteen, and has dropped out of school."

"I claimed I was nineteen." And I was only eighteen – scared and proud – when, her hands on my hips, Marilyn guided me in for my first real sex.

She lifts the glass lid off the chicken pot, gives me a sideways smile, her face instantly rosy from the steam. "So you liked Mayne Island a lot?"

"It's a beautiful part of the world. Most of my time I was just watching the ferry go in and out. But I could imagine us living there in a small house by the sea, with a rowboat."

"I'd hate to be cooped up in the rain inside a dark cabin that's nowhere. Oh, Alex, I told Trevor you would speak to him. He came home drenched on Saturday night, two hours past his curfew. He said he'd just been watching a movie with some friends, but his eyes looked funny."

Playing the heavy is the last thing I feel like doing, after staring closely at blood-stained walls all day. The blood spots were hard to make out on that red wallpa-

74

per with the black design, even though it wasn't raining and the lighting was pretty good.

"You said the murder happened just a few blocks away from here, Alex?"

"566 East 46th Avenue."

"Too close to home."

"Tomorrow I probably have to go back to Mayne Island and …"

"Hi, Daddy-O. When are we going to eat, Mom?"

"Soon. We're just waiting for the potatoes to boil."

"Hi, Trevor." His eyes look normal for him. Ever since his birth, two hours after Lisa, his sky-blue eyes have looked restless. "What you been up to?"

"Nothing much. I went over to a friend's place, and tried to watch the World Series, but game six was rained out, for the third straight time."

"A guy at the station said right field at Fenway was so wet that if a pop fly fell in, you'd need a spoon to dig the ball out of the ground."

"Tiant is scheduled to start tomorrow for the Red Sox."

"He's the only guy who's won for Boston so far. No point saving him for a game seven that might never happen."

"I want Boston to throw a wrench into The Big Red Machine."

"Trevor, could you call Lisa?"

He turns his too-handsome face away from me, and shouts, "LISA!" Trevor turns back to us. "I'm tired of waiting for buses. I want my driver's licence now."

I let Marilyn answer. "I told you when you got your

learner's permit not to expect much use of the family car. Your father takes it to work most of the time, and every second month I need it for when I go on night shift at the hospital."

"Maybe I'll buy my own."

"With what?" I say.

"I could work all weekend at the clothes store if I wanted. The manager likes me a lot."

I intercept Marilyn's glance. "Trevor, I don't want you taking all that time away from your studies. Principal Burns tells us you could have a brilliant future. But it's crucial to do well in school so you can go on to university, and become a lawyer or doctor or whatever you want. I never had that chance."

"Maybe I just want to be a salesman, Dad. Or an actor. Enough with the guilt-trip, OK?"

"Trevor, go knock on Lisa's door, please."

He grabs the newspaper off the counter, spins away, and I am left examining Marilyn's jutting right shoulder blade as she stirs the boiling potatoes.

Lisa appears, somehow taller than I remember.

"Hi, Daddy. You look tired."

"Hi, Pumpkin."

"Lisa, could you set the table please?"

"Why can't Trevor?"

"Because I'm a man."

"Men don't wear red platform shoes."

"They're coo-ol. Freddie Mercury, David Bowie, Mick Jagger, Rod Stewart, all the glam Brits shake their big booties. Glitter rock is in."

"OK, everybody sit down."

"Mom, I'm so happy. Brad invited me to go see Roberta Flack. She's going to be at the Queen Elizabeth Theatre on Halloween Night."

"Killer Queen is where it's at. Who wants to hear schmaltzy croonings about love? 'Killing me softly...'"

"Shut up, Trevor. She sings miles better than Queen. Mom, the performance starts at midnight."

"That's very late. And isn't Brad at university now?"

"He wants to become a surgeon."

"Freddie Mercury is the man."

"You just like him because he dresses up so bizarre."

"Lisa, the whole world is bizarre. Look at the front page of the paper. 'MYSTERY SALMON KILL... More than 1¼ million fish died within 15 minutes at Capilano fish hatchery.' Instead of delivering letters, the postmen are walking off work. '50 KILLED IN MEXICAN SUBWAY CRASH.' And listen to this one: a plumber in West Germany had hiccups for two years, and 'committed suicide by jumping out of a second floor hospital window. Heinz Isecke, 56, got the hiccups in November, 1973, and none of the 3,000 cures which were proposed to him – including gargling with soapy water and swallowing gun oil – cured him.' What's the lesson here? Was the guy lucky or unlucky to die from a leap that was only two floors up?"

"Trevor, your brain's too hyperactive."

"That's redundant."

"Lisa, I will discuss Brad's invitation with your father, but midnight seems very late. And if you're not eating anymore, would you take your plate to the sink."

"That's unfair. Trevor gets to stay out late."

"I'm thinking of changing my name to Frank. Lisa, it's different for guys."

"Guys don't hide a box of rice in their bedroom."

"So that's where my box went!"

"Trevor, what the hell for?" I can't believe what he does sometimes.

"'It's not easy having a good time.' The *Rocky Horror Picture Show*."

"The *Rocky Horror Picture Show*?"

"One of my friends has seen it seventeen times. It opens with huge blood-red lips singing against a black background. You see shiny white teeth, a pink tongue, and glistening saliva threads . . . "

"Gross!"

"Son, some of us are still trying to eat dinner. Marilyn, this chicken is great."

"Well, I was asked. And there's a detective in a tux telling the story on camera who starts dancing to printed-out dance steps. And a lame character named Brad, with tartans and nerdy glasses, who proposes to Janet in a graveyard, and co-ool creatures of the night like Magenta and Riffraff, but I dress up as Dr. Frank N. Furter."

We've all stopped eating.

"This guy on a motorcycle, played by Meatloaf, comes out of the deep freeze, and his corpse ends up under the dinner table, at what Brad and Janet don't know yet is a cannibalistic feast."

"But why did you take my box of rice?"

"Audience participation. It's like a fun party everyone's invited to. You dress up as whoever you want to be, go stand beside the screen, and wait for your character to appear in the movie – then come alive and dance. It's easy having a good time."

"But what's the rice for?"

"To throw at the screen when Dr. Frank N. Furter gets married to his sci-fi creation, Rocky."

"I don't get it."

"Doesn't the theatre manager get upset? Who cleans up the mess?"

"On-Duty Cop Grills Suspect Like an Over-done Chicken. Probes for soft pinky spots in the meat."

"It's just too weird."

"Marilyn, thank you for a very delicious meal. Trevor, you and I will wash up for a change."

"Quick exit, stage left, Lisa. You're supposed to be my *sister*, not my snitcher."

"Trevor, that performance was unacceptable."

"Just gaudy costumes, a little make-up, music to dance to, and a plot as unlikely as life."

How can he still surprise me? "Do you want to wash or dry?"

"I want to act up."

I did too. "Catch this dish towel. Listen, Trevor, I've never told Marilyn this, but when I got my very first paycheque as a cop, you know what I bought?"

"A hunting rifle?"

"No."

"Dad, I want to be splendid. Not a pale moon in a tight orbit that steals a teeny bit of another body's brightness. I want to be the sun, giving off light, sending out rays in all directions."

"I'm listening."

"You've seen me throw a baseball straight and true across the diamond, but I prefer the actual jewellery. And I'm scared of what I want."

"I know, son."

"What are you telling me? What do you mean?"

"You forgot to dry this one. The best part of being made detective was being able to get out of uniform."

"But . . . " He is speechless for once.

"All I'm saying is in life you sometimes don't get to choose your costume."

"And . . . "

What can I say? "I'm your father, always."

Skin

skin
clown's coat
film that bruises and sags with age
spectrum of odours
continuous death and renewal
universe's limits
incredible fine mesh of danger
most vulnerable prison
(and everyone one of us
some times would sell life
for the intimate
touch of skin)
filter and mask and ultimate
test of truth
skin mimics history
dictates its own continent
most divisive and most
unifying theatre
our only meeting place
skin is what learns
and teaches us our lives

• Pat Lowther

Saturday morning, October 18, 1975

How do you survive love? Or the man with blue hair?
No longer surprised by sin.

Sandra once rode me across the back yard, jerking
the fresh-tasting blue plastic in my mouth. Mad about
horses, she used my new skipping rope for reins. Love?
Hate? When I whimpered, she just wrapped a scarf
around the bit, yelled "giddy-up," and rode on, remak-
ing my mouth. How did I survive my big sister's passion for horses? I fell in the deep grass and refused to
get back up on all fours. She told me I had been adopted.

Saved by Grannie on the phone when I was five or
six, "Lindie, you sound *just* like your mother." I felt
reborn, became a nervy kid.

Eleven when I tested my new-found power of handwriting, and made out a twenty dollar cheque to
Sandra, carefully copying Mom's signature. I put it in
an envelope with a flowery card as a surprise Easter
present. When Sandra cashed it, and bought the new

82

Beatles album and a large poster of a galloping black horse, I was half-scared of her swift and sure punishment – but longed to see my mother's face curdle in Deep Disappointment and to hear my father's voice boom with Righteous Wrath. Waited through days and weeks of nothing because my parents never found out, or could not face the notion of sin in our own family.

When Nigel drove me back here to his place from The Body Shop Discotheque, in his dark blue Jaguar XKE, I avoided looking down at the bed. Instead, I focused on the black shine of an abstract painting, an inky Rorschach lake, which, if I were lucky, I thought, might turn into night magic. I kissed the stranger with the lovely British accent and had trouble breathing. As if one of my lungs had collapsed. Fell back on his wide futon, my glasses still on, and watched his electric blue head circle and bob between my legs. That sinful kiss of me down there. When he gently rolled me over, a dozen cacti, bulbous and prickly, stared at me from the window sill, while he took me from behind, horsie fashion.

Surprised by Sin: the Reader in Paradise Lost, by Stanley Fish.

I need to finish the Milton essay by Tuesday. At least I've got an extension on that short story from Professor Williams. Yesterday, he didn't want to talk with a mere student about a colleague's murder, but I had something important to show him, a copy of a poem Professor Lowther had given me in our tutorial:

"To a woman who died of 34 stab wounds." Did she intuit what was coming?

Concentrate on the Milton paper, Lindie. Fish argues that the meaning of the poem is to be found in the reader's experience of it.

Yesterday morning, Nigel ran towards me with his bouncey bits, and spoke in a Professor Higgins voice, "I say, you realize it doesn't wear out from overuse." Came again, like a shuddering camel in the desert. Right after, he told me he was flying to Bangkok – a name that always is a joke for guys – so I wasn't sure what he meant, or what to believe.

Fish.

> [T]he true center of *Paradise Lost* is the reader's consciousness of the poem's *personal* relevance, and that the arc of the poem describes, in addition to the careers of the characters, the education of its readers. This education proceeds in two stages: in the first, the reader is brought face to face with the corruption within him [her], as [s]he is made aware of the confusion reigning in his [her] scale of values and of the inadequacy of his [her] perceptions; in the second, [s]he is invited to cooperate with the poem's effort to effect [her]his regeneration. . . .

A house key in my palm, as Nigel drove off to the airport in his XKE. *Blaue reiter* – my blue rider. Reader.

Fish says the form of the reader's experience of Milton's *Paradise Lost* leads to righteousness, but I embraced Nigel Poole instead of the Supreme Good.

[T]he outer or physical form, so obtrusive, and, in one sense, so undeniably there, is, in another sense, incidental and even irrelevant.

No longer is the poem an object of reverence as it was for my dear dead Grannie, a shining gem in this mortal and flawed world. Her puffy fingers would turn the pages of Keats as if they were edged with eternity. Now, forget the poem as a verbal icon, ignore the radiant words, mock the music of rhymes, laugh at the earlier generations hungry for Beauty and Truth. We all live in Rorschach now. This self-centred place where our reactions become the meaning: only the lights exploding inside the skull matter. Even the hard sinful gleam of Nigel's body becomes incidental, irrelevant. Like toked-out hippies, whatever turns you on, man.

"The very essence of Truth is plainnesse, and brightnes; the darknes and crookednesse is our own."

Tomorrow's Sunday. I could go to the Lutheran chapel on campus. I have an urge to kneel, pray, this pain in my chest to release.

From Nigel's kitchen window I can see Passage Island and the sun on the calm waters of the Inlet, and it looks paradisal. He said I might as well stay in his newly painted pad for a couple of weeks, at least while he was away in Asia. It's so much better here than shivering in a dank, spidery room half-below the damp ground of University Hill.

There's the phone. It must be for Nigel, so I'll let it ring.

[It] dictates a reorientation of the debate con-
cerning the structure or form of the poem;
for if the meaning of the poem is to be located in the reader's experience of it, the form
of the poem is the form of that experience. . . .

What if I tried to read Pat Lowther's poem that
way? It must still be in a pocket of my black pants
that I hung up in Nigel's closet. I told her some kitschy
thing about getting eye-strain from trying to glimpse
the Muse, and that all I ended up seeing were teary
shadows sliding over marble eyeballs. Some Gothic
drivel like that. She just tilted her head, pressed her
pale forehead with her thumb and ring finger, and gave
me a look, along with a recent poem, "To a woman
who died of 34 stab wounds."

My favourite two lines: "Your heavy scarlet smile /
held out like a credit card." None of her words strained
to do too much.

It's hard to ignore a ringing phone with its perpetual
question: Who's attached to the other end of the um-
bilical cord? The cord that nourishes and sometimes
strangles. I know my God-fearing mother back in
Abbotsford doesn't have Nigel's number. Hard to believe the pious dairy farmers of the Fraser Valley are
less than an hour's drive away from this profane city,
its university of dangerous ideas on the edge of a cliff.
Mom would be horrified to know I've been living in
sin with a man with blue hair.

Dr. Jones told me that blue babies, sometimes have
the birth cord wrapped around their neck. But I had a
congenital heart defect. Bluish lips. Needed corrective
surgery.

There's the phone again, and I haven't written anything on Milton yet. *Paradise Lost* is hard enough to figure out without sorting through what Stanley Fish has to say about it.

Nigel has very few books. Three rows of yellow-backed National Geographic magazines, and a tall navy-blue *Canadian Oxford Atlas*.

The phone – like a skipping rope, to play with, to trip up, one person at each end, waiting for something to jump into the sing-song turnings.

My previous boyfriend Tim turned huffy because I gave my cousin a hug in the bookstore. Prickled and puffed with jealousy – sharp invisible thorns popped out of his hairy male skin. Was I supposed to act like a martyr, stroke away his foolish hurts with bleeding fingers? He stopped phoning, avoided me on campus. Wanted me to be a shy virgin sex maniac. His idea of love-making was the mechanics of moving parts: steel piston inside a lubricated cylinder. He had no shoulders to fill out his red Engineering jacket, but tossed me away like scrap metal. Wreckage to be picked over by someone else in a junkyard.

Definitely was in the dumps when I met Nigel. At the Discotheque I had to stop myself from climbing onto him and squeezing his narrow waist with my legs.

Bangkok. I tug out the atlas, and turn to "The Gazetteer." Thailand: 64 C4. Flip some pages and there, on the soft green of sea level, near the Gulf of Siam, not too far from Vietnam, is a black dot inside a small circle. Who is that blue-haired man? And why is someone again calling him so insistently? On a whim, I thumb back to "The Gazetteer" and look under "R." And there actually turns out to be such a place, in neutral Switzerland. At the southern end of Lake Constance, the town of Rorschach.

Hefting the atlas upright from the table, I fan the pages, hoping to see some document flutter out. But nothing falls free. All there is is a dedication, inscribed near the top of the title page in blue-black ink in a woman's looped left hand, "To Nigel, on the occasion of our first wedding anniversary, with perfect love, Barbara."

I'm a blue baby again, with deoxygenated blood in my arteries. Nigel and Barbara Poole. *Paradise Lost*. You let a blue-haired man pick you up at a disco and expect true love? A congenital brain defect.

When I snatch at the phone, I get only a dial tone. A port or resort or trading post or whatever, Rorschach is where we live our blobby lives.

I go into his bedroom, start searching. In Nigel's closet, next to my pants with the Pat Lowther poem, are a dozen billowy silk shirts: ivory, cream, and pale blue. On the top shelf, where I can't quite reach, a shoebox full of photographs. By my feet, a pair of polished boots which appear unworn, one cracked leather sandal, and some cheap black running shoes with an eyelet missing.

Too impatient to drag over a chair, I jump, grab at the box of photos, but miss. I leap a second time and manage to pinch the cardboard corner, and topple everything over, down on top of me. Like Milton's Samson Agonistes pulling down the Temple of the

Unrighteous around me. Sticking to my clothes and skin are photos of smiling women, in bikinis, more often topless, a few completely naked, and, almost always, Nigel's arm around their bare shoulders. I brush the images off myself, and begin to sift through the disorderly piles of pictures. Some I turn over like dreaded cards in Hearts. Who photographed all these women snuggling next to him? An automatic timer? Their breasts white, black, pink, tan, replaceable. And in nearly every picture, under a blonde Beatles cut, Nigel grins.

> *It took her awhile to grow used to the gloom*
> *behind the forbidden door. It took some time*
> *to figure out that her feet were sticking to*
> *the floor with clotted blood. It took a minute*
> *to realize that she was now among the bod-*
> *ies of the women Bluebeard had murdered.*

Get a grip, Lindie. The man has blue hair, not a beard. A Chevalier, though, a rider of horses. And several of the women in the photos wear on their left hand what looks like the same bloated, glassy diamond. In my fairy tale of rescue the prince with satin shirts has turned into a villain.

My hands rush together his happy, teeth-filled images: impossible to put them back in the right order in the shoebox.

One isolated snapshot shows a squinting woman with braids that are dripping with water. I pick it up, and discover underneath her image a tiny manila envelope. Written on its back, in Barbara Poole's elegant hand, "Royal Bank, 10th & Sasamat." Inside, I can feel a thin key.

> *She snatched it out of the pooled blood and ran to the sink where the key stained with blood wouldn't rinse off. She tried more soap, but still the redness remained. She scrubbed desperately with sandstone. Never would the blood come off.*

Dull metal with only a few notches, and a hollow head. Drilled or stamped out, designed to hold vacant air: indeterminacy. The bank branch is close by, on the way back to my basement room out at UBC. The safety deposit key in my hand feels like a Temptation.

> *The key to the forbidden room fell from her hand.*

I quickly shove all the photos into the shoebox.

That night Bluebeard unexpectedly returns?

Is there a bluish coloration around my lips? I drag the wooden chair over, step up on it and push the box of disordered images way back on the shelf, against the wall.

> *He commanded his wife to fetch the missing key.*

The small weighted envelope slips into my pocket. My pair of black pants are slung over an arm, and the closet's fanfold door closed tight.

> *Weeping, she pleaded at Bluebeard's feet for a few minutes of prayer.*

90

My prayers of rescue, someone to watch over me? Gershwin. More like someone to walk over me, or giddy-up.

> Two horsemen rushed in with swords upraised, and thrust them right through Bluebeard's body.

In this International Women's Year, I have no brothers.

I drop *Surprised by Sin* into my briefcase. Carefully, I remove Patricia Lowther's double-folded poem from my pants pocket, and tuck it alongside the hard blue cloth that covers Milton's bulky text. She wrote in some anthology that even the most hostile and fearful women were absorbing liberation from imposed self-images along with cream depilatory commercials. A sardonic hope? I lift up my briefcase.

> *Moral: Curiosity leads to regret.*

For Bluebeard's wives, for Eve, for Linda Hanson. Running, I pull my raincoat off a hanger and thrust my free arm through a sleeve, throw my purse over the wrong shoulder, and open the door to the outside. No XKE is parked by the curb. With a bang of my knee, I shut the door to Nigel's castle.

Overcast now, but not raining. I walk rapidly away, scared at how my own body, stupid with sinful desires, has betrayed me again. I have a hollow head, like that safety deposit key: vacant, fatuous. "Infatuation," what you call love afterwards. "False glisterings."

How could I be surprised? A mis-reading, a missed reading, a sentimental "miss" reading? Does all interpretation have a gender bias? Then humans can share no ikons. "Bi-assed," a word I've never understood: everyone's bottom has two fleshy parts. Any theory that tells us only personal experience is true has to be fishy. Go Fish! I wonder if Pat Lowther ever played that game. Did she try again and again to find the right card, only to accumulate, finally, unplayable ones?

I wanted love to be a kind of co-conspiracy – part of a secret plan to fool the world into happiness: "a film of *ignorance.*" Our two bodies coming together in delight and Blakean daring, but maybe just horniness, or a longing for *de-repression* ...

A grey-bearded man, holding a black and white puppy on a leash, scrutinizes me. Did I speak that last word out loud? Giving myself away, again. As I move past him, the dog jumps up at its owner, front paws scrabbling at his belt.

At the bus stop, I read the headlines in the smudgy window of the metal box:

WHELAN THREATENS ROLL-
BACK ON FOOD PRICES

WOMAN GANGLAND BOSS

Unzipping my purse, I find some coins and drop them in with soft clunks. Pulling down the springy door, I lift out a newspaper as the 10th Avenue bus wheezes to a stop. I'm searching through the pages as I step on – showing the bored driver my pass when I read

SLAIN VANCOUVER POET
WROTE OF BLOODY DEATH,
by Michael Finlay

I collapse into an aisle seat.

> "The thought of one's own death
> lies in a crypt of mind, like a
> palmed egg. It lies couched in a
> hammock of blood."

I have to get off very soon if I'm going to do it.

> On Monday, her badly decom-
> posed body was hauled from
> Furry Creek near Britannia
> Beach. Detectives investigating
> the case as a murder say they
> have a suspect in mind but no ar-
> rest is imminent.

The next stop. I shouldn't.

> "She was star-crossed."

There's the Varsity theatre. Lindie, don't do it.

> " . . . equal of Margaret Atwood
> and Gwendolyn MacEwan."

I step down, off, onto a hill crowded with shoppers. In front of Hewer's Hardware, the display of umbrellas reminds me I left mine at Bluebeard's. Tempted by the yeasty smells wafting from the Golden Sheaf, I pause.

But looming, on the north-west corner of the intersection of 10th & Sasamat, the Royal Bank. Pray for my soul. No, you are a hypocrite, Lindie. Why are you always arguing with me? Because you are like a whited sepulchre. No, I'm the young woman held in a closet for a month, code-name Tania, with a loaded gun in her purse. Lindie, behave like a good young Christian woman, my mother would say.

93

Bumped from behind, I move forward on the dark grey concrete, each of my steps bringing me closer to Sin. Watch a station wagon turn the corner, then I cross over.

Enter the bank, and my heart beats as if I am in love.

"Yes?"

I touch at my glasses. "I'd like to see my safety deposit box, please."

"Your name?"

I put the newspaper and black pants down on the hard-edged counter. "Barbara Poole."

The teller stands, pivots away in her tight grey skirt. She pulls out a filing cabinet drawer, riffles through some cards, and takes one out, places it before me, Linda Hanson, Honours English student with a Minor in Creative Writing, who's supposed to be writing fiction, not living it. I pick the ballpoint pen out of its cupped holder, find its balance point, and with a glance at one of the two signatures at the top of the card, copy smoothly.

The teller looks down, then up at my face fast. Extending her arm, she unlocks the low swinging gate. A row of dark blue buttons down the side of her skirt. I pass through the entrance, in a state of grace.

I give her the small manila envelope.

But first she uses one of the keys on her metal hoop, while I try to hide my troubled breathing.

Then she takes out my key, which really has only two dimensions, and belongs to Nigel's wife's (who can't possibly look like me?). The small, thick steel door is flung back, and I see the end of a metal box: dull army-green.

The teller slips my key inside the tiny envelope, and holds it out to me – as if it were a communion wafer.

A choking sensation in my throat.

Her hips swivel, and I count seven hard skirt buttons as she scrapes out the long rectangle.

Proffers it. Take this.

Its slidey weight rocks gently on the skin of my hand.

Riding Past

Long street of houses
with lighted roofs
black against

winter sky blue as Venetian glass
with Venus hanging
like a small yellow moon

In the houses people
are cooking food and scolding children
the ones home from work

are hanging their coats up
telephones are ringing
behind the yellow windows

Come, open the doors
yellow rectangles and steam
of meat and potatoes

Stand on the front steps
stare at the sky and wave
Look, we're riding past Venus

• Pat Lowther

Friday afternoon, October 17, 1975

The light fading, yet still here. Why hasn't Moira, my green and lovely fate, called as promised? Jane, my not-quite ex, phones more often. Yesterday, it was about Willie not coming home the night before.

The time before that it was about some triangular ruler Willie had swiped. It's hard to imagine why. And I am supposed to do what? Since I slid out of the house in mid-August, my son won't talk to me.

I pull the newspaper towards me.

RECORD RAINS BRING 1
DEATH AND FLOODING

This morning I wouldn't have been surprised to see a salmon swimming up the street.

> The almost continuous downpour began to taper off at 8 a.m. today as the intense storm passed inland. Heavy rain caused two rockslides in the Fraser Can-

97

yon that blocked the Trans-
Canada Highway briefly early
today.

Feels like a rock-slide happened in my skull, block-
ing any useful thought pathway. I should give up trying to write a chunk of my own fiction and just grab
another story off that ungraded stack. Creative Writh-
ing. Let my tired brain limp after an obvious plot. Be
grateful (for once) for the dead thud of syntax and a
predictable ending. But boredom never soothes. Won't
dull my edginess this afternoon. And (too often?) in
student fiction-making I glimpse a raw newness that
scares the hell out of me. Two years without a publication. Blocked.

TEACHERS RIDE TO RESCUE
OF NEW YORK (AP)

New York's chances of avoiding
immediate financial disaster im-
proved today when the teachers'
union president reversed his position and recommended that the
union commit $150 million of its
retirement fund to help bail out
the city.

So American, that metaphor. Teachers as the US
cavalry galloping in at the last moment to save a des-
perate situation. The same metaphor that got them
into Vietnam. Willie doesn't want to be rescued. A kid
who always ran full-tilt out into the rain.

BODY IDENTITY CONFIRMED

Homicide detectives have posi-

> tively identified the body found
> last week near Squamish as
> missing poet Pat Lowther, 40,
> who disappeared from her Van-
> couver home.

No. Too horrible. Pat murdered, and seven years younger than me.

> She had apparently been killed
> by a head blow which fractured
> . . . .

"Professor Williams?"

A young woman, all in black, stands just outside my office. "Yes?"

"Your door was open and I just thought . . . "

What's her name? She takes my Tuesday afternoon workshop. Fixes the glasses on her face and looks for words.

"I guess I was wondering if you had . . . "

I must look impatient, wanting to read the bad bad news about Pat's murder.

She glances down at the newspaper on my desk, then lifts up a bold, diamond-shaped face.

"What is it?"

"I want an extension on our first fiction assignment. I don't have an excuse."

"Can't you make up a good story?" A beat, then she giggles, a hand reaching for her slightly parted mouth. "OK. Until a week Tuesday."

"Thanks."

Her black pants turn and she is gone.

> . . . disappeared from her Van-

couver home on Sept. 24.

She had apparently been killed by a head blow which fractured her skull.

The badly decomposed remains, pulled out of Furry Creek on Monday. . . .

I'll probably have to testify. I can imagine the dialogue.

Q   *An organized meeting was once a week?*

A   *Yes, that's – well, she was hired to come one full day a week, which would be Thursday. She was to be here from approximately nine in the morning through till about five at night. She would do a workshop from 10:30 to 12:30. She would do tutorials before and after that workshop. . . .*

Detectives said they have a suspect in mind and will be questioning the person. However, they added that an arrest is not imminent.

Q   *And when you phoned, a man answered the phone, I gather.*

A   Yes.

Q   *And what did he say?*

A   *Well, first of all, he sounded very, very*

sleepy, and then I said who I was and
then he immediately became very
much wide awake.

Q   *Yes?*

Investigators Thursday left
Mayne Island after spending two
days talking with the victim's
husband, Roy, 42. He moved into
a cabin on the island with two of
the couple's children shortly after his wife's disappearance.

A   *On the Thursday morning when she*
should have been teaching at UBC,
which would be about 10:30 in the
morning, she would have started her
class, he said she had phoned him to
say she was going east. And I, you
know, I couldn't quite get what this
meant, so I simply asked the question,
you know, "Where east?" And then he
said, "Oh, just east." It seemed rather a
vague direction that she'd gone in
according to him and so eventually he
said, "Well, Frank, this is a triangular
affair." I remember that as being a
phrase that he used, and I was a little
astounded at this, to say the least.

Pat's shy face flitted between prettiness and beauty.
Her scarf had designs like butterfly wings.

"The Face." The name of her prose poem that I pro-
foundly envied when it came out in *Prism* last year.

Jane would always reassure me about the importance of my own work, but what's a wife supposed to say? That her husband from picturesque Pouch Cove, Newfoundland, is only a bit player in the Canadian cultural renaissance, with barely a speaking part? That the boyo from the Rock who turned one thin Dylan Thomasesque book into careerism is a competent teacher and administrator?

Pat's voice could be so quiet it was like being brushed by the knobbed antennae of a butterfly.

From the top bookshelf, I get down our department journal, the spring 1974 issue of *Prism*:

THE FACE
Pat Lowther

1. THE FACE
Always when I wake my first consciousness is of your face, inside me, as it were under my own, as if my features overlay yours. In those first moments the face is stylized, the hair and beard curled like those of statues. Only gradually, as I move, you move too, the face becomes individual.

I do not recall having dreamt of you. I cast back into sleep: a heavy vacancy, neither of us was there.

All faces change minute to minute. Aspects of your face accompany me, changing without waiting for my intention. I do not invent you. The photograph you sent me has an aspect which has occupied me less than others. I must bring it into balance with your other faces.

The face in the photograph is impressive, formidable in fact. The man with that face, I say to myself, can *cope*. That man will always have everything under control. I am perhaps intimidated.

Most often I remember your face close up, foolish-loving, looking much younger. Or with eyes closed kissing, the even tension of shut eyelids, a sheen like wing cases, a detail giving disproportionate pleasure.

But at my first waking I think we are both eyeless, with the brutal dignity of ancient masks. I imagine myself thin and gold, my hands locked at my sides, tongue locked to the roof of my mouth, each hair root locked in its pore. I imagine myself a sarcophagus carried to burial, an image of you static as a photograph locked under my face.

2. THE CLOTHING

You are so much more clothed than I am. Underwear top and bottom, everything tucked in. I could never touch your body by accident. I could never in a casual embrace slide my hand onto skin and body hair. You have to undress first.

And you carry your life like clothing too. It's very becoming, it suits you. Your relationships with the people around you look good, their textures are interesting. You are conscious of origins.

Maybe you have it all worked out: just enough pain and struggle to allow you to keep the nerve ends vibrating. Enough disorder to have let you fall in love with me.

I have a longing now to stare at your real face, to question, demand to know you. But you were the one who stared that way into my face. All the time we were together your eyes never left me, I couldn't eat or sleep. And when you asked me to tell you about my life, so that you could picture what I'd be doing at different hours of the day, I wouldn't answer you.

Listen: every morning I take a razor to the fabric of my life, I cut out a woman shape, I step into it, I go out, I perform, it works. But every morning it has to be done again.

Sometimes I can't get the blade sharp enough, the shape flat enough. I can't manage a protoplasm silhouette one molecule thick.

My shape takes exaggerated depth like those optical-illusion letters they use to advertise religious movies, where the edges go back and back into the page and come together at a point representing infinity. My continuum drags behind me, a rubble of dark and rough and glitter stretching back probably to the point of birth.

Then my whole life seems like the act of birth, as violent and difficult and inescapable. My clothing is bloody membrane and sea water, dragging at my body.

I can't even imagine what you feel like in your turtleneck sweater, checkered pants, tidy underwear.

3. THE MACHINERY

The machinery is, in abstract, like a space wheel in orbit. Stately precise turning into and out of sunlight.

If we were separate from it, it would seem lovely. We would breathe in delight seeing it in a movie.

The machine is, of course, a centrifuge. We're locked on its outside walls by the magnetic soles of our feet, the veins branching downwards. I think of a glass anatomical model of a man, with an erection.

As if the earth had gone transparent and its gross axis become visible, turning us. Like a drill-core spectrum, a blackened rainbow, the red orange yellow at the centre, further toward the ends roughness, jumble, glisten of coal and oil pools, moving capillaries of water. The ends themselves hard glossy white, ice that never melts. The effortless spin of the thing generating so much brute power.

Sometimes I think I can see you across the curvature of the walls. We might reach out, try to touch.

But the machine holds us motionless. Our muscles flatten, our veins and arteries spread out like maps. We are splayed, pinned down on separate beds, in separate cities.

I'm turning downward into sleep. I will not dream of you. Slowly, slowly, it's turning you toward your morning. You are beginning to remember me.

My legs tired, I sit down, and start crowding pencil notes into the blank spaces around Pat's words.

THE FACE [not "my" or" his" or "your" or "a" or "our": the definite article specifies the identifiable that here is left to vagueness, and lost to connotations of deception]

1. THE FACE

Always when I wake [fidelity and newness] *my first* ["always" and "first," both words of impossible purity, with Romantic insistence on intensity, with the diction of Leonard Cohen] *consciousness is of your face, inside me,* [conventional sentiment given metaphysical twist after the comma of invasive horror, plus sexual wish (by choosing "me" instead of "mine") with presence made larger than face surface – implies whole body, and a paradoxical interiority of outward visage] *as it were under my own,* [a partial correction of previous phrase, and suggestion of underlying optics, screening out the other's sight of world for something deeper, yet also the politics of power and dependency] *as if my features overlay yours.* [speaker reclaims sense of equality with "overlay," and makes her own face into a mask , all in one sentence, where declarative assertion, "Always when I wake my first consciousness is . . . ," becomes hypothetical, "as it were," "as if," with a fact claimed now openly exposed as imagined, showing the metaphor in act of giving face to impression; this first sentence could be broken up into half a dozen short lines, and be a poem in itself] *In those first moments* [repetition here paradoxically signifying start] *the face is stylized,* [whose? – momentary loss of referent, which is appropriate since both faces are overlapped and overlapping; sense of design, of conscious style, at a remove from everyday acceptance of facial appearance as biologically given] *the hair and beard* [a male addressed here] *curled like those of statues.* [the human face as sculpted art: immobile,

106

inanimate and heavy with convention] *Only gradu-*
ally, as I move, you move too, [a disequilibrium of self
makes statue come to life, a Pygmalion trip wherein a
woman artist shapes a male into a desired form and is
moved by her own creating; love of others as a self-
deception, or, more convoluted, falling in love as an
act of self-hypnosis in which one's wished for, com-
plimentary self is given a complementary visible
body to believe in // Moira, who flatters me with her
youth, her appetite for drugs, but mostly it's my own
fantasy of a lovemaking that would be like falling out
of a window from one of the wooden shacks that cling
to the high stone cliff above Pouch Cove, Newfound-
land] *the face becomes individual.* [but which one of
the overlapping visages is in the act of separating out
a self?; also, if "the" includes both "your" and "I" in shared
process of particularizing a face, then "individual" becomes tinged with the social, the external, the false front
// with Moira, an aging man's exciting fiction that, in
reality, is no more than the usual sliding friction]

I do not recall having dreamt of you. I cast back
into sleep: a heavy vacancy, [oxymoron of weighted
absence // still waiting here for my absent Moira //
the memoryless quality of most sleep that's necessary
for the artist-dreamer as Pygmalion, since to believe
in love is to forget all knowledge of having made a
"cast": a word offering three metaphorical directions:
sculpting of a statue no more compelling than fishing
for something, or choosing an actor] *neither of us was*
there. [therefore either the dream imagery is repressed
or an awakening to an unimagined beloved, a plot-

line the speaker necessarily distrusts, given its proximity to the wishfulness of fairy tales // can Pat really be dead?]

BODY IDENTITY CONFIRMED

All faces change minute to minute. [not a bronze statue's // but mine, Jane's, Willie's, even Moira's, though she pays no mind to the heavy rain in her face or the noonday sun all over her body at Wreck Beach; Pat reluctant to be photographed, a bit of the Emily Dickinson recluse poetess, though she is – was – Co-Chair of the League of Canadian Poets, but not yet famous like Margaret Atwood who's on every cover, every CBC radio show and TV panel; I'm no shining star in the firmament of Can. Lit., but maybe I contribute a few watts to its mass and brightness; should be happy to glow like the palest of stars in Ursa Minor]

I'll begin the paragraph again.

All faces change minute to minute. Aspects of your face accompany me, changing without waiting for my intention. [companionable, but independent, altering without my wish or will, though "aspects" implies the astronomical, the mutual pull of gravity caused by the weight of physical bodies; the addressed becoming the dependent moon?] *I do not invent you.* [assertion as negation, insisting (naively?) on an other beyond subjective contrivance and desires] *The photograph you sent me has an aspect which has occupied me less than others.* [those facets or appearances given selective preference in her memory among the multiple and mutable looks of a face, or aspects of other faces, beloveds; "occupied" suggests a conquering army, and given initiating metaphor of "inside me," not only a psychological preoccupation or mental residence, but also physical penetration] *I must bring it into balance with your other faces.* [a Cubist many-sidedness here that offers both fullness and elusiveness, with maybe a hint of accusation about human deceit, even if the speaker as artist intends to reassert control over image-making. First noticed Moira as a teenage skateboarder with cat's eyes, living just five houses away, whom Jane had asked to baby-sit Willie: her white helmet decorated with green electrician tape in a series of plus marks, or plant sprouts, or crosses. Last year, she took my introductory creative writing course, and used the instruction manual for a Briggs & Stratton lawnmower as the plotline of a story, and its diction to convey the mind of a suburban protagonist conscientiously mowing down unruly growth]

The face in the photograph is impressive, formidable in fact. [capable of making an impression, Kafkaesque threat à la "In the Penal Colony" of tattooing the flesh, of imprinting a message under the skin, a surreal and punitive menace underlined by "in fact"] *The man with that face, I say to myself, can cope. That man will always have everything under control. I am perhaps intimidated.* [the kinetics of fears and wishes, an implicit vulnerability that's attracted to (male?) competence and strength, then shifts in a flash-forward to an intimation of unfreedom and dread, though doubt qualifies and offers perspective in a way that is not entirely intimidated]

Most often I remember your face close up, foolish-loving, [subtle alliterative link with "formidable" reverses the power politics at the beginning of this next poetic paragraph; "foolish-loving" revives and revises the lyric of "Why do Fools Fall in Love?" by transposing cause and effect, suggesting our delight in illusion and foolery] *looking much younger.* [and pivots again with praise of youthfulness // the young face in my author's photo that used to be mine, now closer to Willie's // correlation between inexperience and folly, but, more positively, youth pulls us back to the sense of "first" and "wake" in the opening] *Or with eyes closed* [hers aren't – observant] *kissing,* [a spectator even at moment of passion?] *the even tension of shut eyelids,* [perhaps equal between each pair of eyes as well, and maybe a balance of equal blindness] *a sheen like wing cases,* [and in one simile Pat makes vivid my imagining, with her very fine image of incipient flight, of ecstasy-in-waiting // Moira! //for me a briefcase of unfinished stories and the shitload of student papers to mark up] *a detail giving disproportionate pleasure.* [a wariness about the distortions of love, emphasis on physical sensations through "pleasure," and an avoidance of its more abstract synonyms, "joy" and "happiness"]

But at my first waking I think we are both eyeless, with the brutal dignity of ancient masks. [blurs two opposite categories, the comic and the tragic that masks are supposed to distinguish for those seated faraway in the amphitheatre, unable to see the actors' faces, oxymoron tells of our condition: the dignifying of brutes, the turning of prose into poetry] *I imagine myself thin and gold, my hands locked at my sides, tongue locked to the roof of my mouth, each hair root locked in its pore.* [the statue again, where hair and beard never grow, and a muteness in which even gestures of hands are imprisoned ("locked" three times), maybe in a social pose beyond anyone's making] *I imagine myself a sarcophagus carried to burial, an image of you static as a photograph locked under my face.* [in ending this section she returns to opening except now hides and holds in a context that's not waking but burial // I should contact the League of Canadian Poets about helping organize a memorial service.]

2. THE CLOTHING

You are so much more clothed than I am. Underwear top and bottom, everything tucked in. I could never touch your body by accident. [implies protected and inaccessible; maybe a wish thwarted by geographical distance or by fear of rejection due to Wilhelm Reich "armouring"; neatness as social virtue became a put-down in the late 60s, a badge of conformity, deference, and criminal obedience during the Vietnam War // Moira's clothes an endless self-sculpting: a Cubist Pygmalion creating not a Galatea but hundreds of Pygmalion selves instead] *I could never in a casual embrace slide my hand onto skin and body hair. You have to undress first.* [observation as accusation becomes, in this last short sentence, negotiation or command]

And you carry your life like clothing too. [this analogy of the dress-up-able points to the speaker's fear of being put-off-able, discardable.] *It's very becoming, it suits you.* [joke-y pun has a kind of source in Plath's "Daddy"?] *Your relationships with the people around you look good, their textures are interesting.* [cliché compliment about appearance shows distrust in the weaving of relationships, but also holds out multiple possibilities of becoming, not fixed to any single aspect, thus linking sections 1 and 2] *You are conscious of origins.* [contradicts previous sentence where all connections are superficial? // my brain is getting tired // maybe Pat means an awareness of costume and casting, an anticipation of the social performance of self in the act of becoming; it's getting too muddy for me; where are her cleansing metaphors?]

Maybe you have it all worked out: [I don't; does she mean <u>everything</u> here? – the origins of life itself, our huge gaping universe, or just neat everyday answers, like Hemingway for much of his life, on what to wear, where to go, who to drink with, how to seek out danger and not lose control] *just enough pain and struggle to allow you to keep the nerve ends vibrating.* [what an accusation! such a fine-tuning of feelings is monstrous, normal // me? a post-adolescent lifetime of emotional and sensory control, keeping out overload and avoiding power failure, until Moira and disorder beckoned – but no longer call?] *Enough dis-*

order to have let you fall in love with me. [a shrewd, unsentimental definition of love as managed chaos, though here she accuses him of coolly measuring out volts of emotions, calculating what's needed to maintain his electrical circuitry // my passion for Moira half out of boredom, a wish to induce family catastrophe, financial bleakness, creative angst?]

I have a longing now to stare at your real face, to question, demand to know you. But you were the one who stared that way into my face. [mostly by accident, I had body-checked Jane, then had fallen on top of her, and had scrutinized the pain in her face. We were just a few boyos in grade eleven playing street hockey with a fuzzless tennis ball when a trio of grade nine girls had strolled by, wanting to play. My fall had broken Jane's arm. I was very contrite, even before her mother chewed me out. I asked Jane to the Saturday night movie. She seemed happy, walking to the pictures with a shiny cast on her arm. Still feel badly for what I did to her] ... *you were the one who stared that way into my face. All the time we were together your eyes never left me, I couldn't eat or sleep. And when you asked me to tell you about my life, so that you could picture what I'd be doing at different hours of the day, I wouldn't answer you.* [a self-protective refusal of the other's pseudo-omniscient gaze; this paragraph almost the entire prose poem in miniature]

Listen: every morning I take a razor to the fabric of my life, [face and clothing, metaphorical sources of parts 1 and 2 brought together as surreal destruction, with maybe an ironic allusion to Penelope who each night unweaves her tapestry, renewing her fidelity] *I cut out a woman shape,* [feminist consciousness plays with domestic imagery of dressmaking, but the razor conveys desperation // and is probably <u>not</u> an ironic echo of the Moerae, the three Greek goddesses who spin the web of life into cloth, measure its length, and cut out its shape: just my obsession with Moira] *I step into it, I go out, I perform, it works.* [like Atwood's poem, "On the streets, love," where all is social role and costume, with "perform" pointing back to theatre and ancient masks] *But every morning it has to be done again.* [waking again to perform the perpetual social task of falseness; R. D. Laing stuff, especially about women distorting themselves to act as flattering mirrors to men // not Moira – as selfish as us]

Sometimes I can't get the blade sharp enough, the shape flat enough. [two-dimensional social ideal, and a reprise of "I imagine myself thin"] *I can't manage a protoplasm silhouette one molecule thick.* [technical terms of biology and chemistry in context of love like the metaphysical conceits of Donne, and a reminder of an evolved animal body and brain that can't retreat from its complexity]

My [dubious possessive singular] *shape takes exaggerated depth like those optical-illusion letters they use to advertise religious movies, where the edges go back and back into the page and come together at a point representing infinity.* [claim for more than a two-dimensional fullness with a hip use of pop culture, like Beats, by borrowing quirky details from urban landscape; funny and perceptive about advertising with its sense of hype and fraud – especially here with graphics promising the infinite and everlasting if you buy a ticket to watch cinematic images of salvation or damnation] *My continuum drags behind me, a rubble of dark and rough* [vague and weak posture of black romanticism?] *and glitter* [but rescues with the third parallel noun, which surprises, like sparks off pavement as a muffler drags] *stretching back probably to the point* [time or position <u>and</u> underlying meaning, if any] *of birth.*

Then my whole life seems like the act of birth, as violent and difficult and inescapable. [passive perspective of one who can't intervene to alter anything: fated] *My clothing is bloody membrane and sea water, dragging at my body.* ["The badly decomposed remains, pulled out of Furry Creek . . . "]

I can't even imagine what you feel like in your turtleneck [animal with protective shell // like me, perhaps, with a steady job and a mortgaged house to retreat back into] *sweater, checkered pants, tidy underwear.* [mocking him, resenting him, implicitly asking, Why am I attracted to one so unlike me? // my fantasy experience with Moira who isn't going to call]

3. THE MACHINERY
The machinery is, in abstract, like a space wheel in orbit. [like Lowry's Máquina Infernal, the Ferris wheel in *Under the Volcano* that revolves with festive infernal determinism?] *Stately precise turning into and out of sunlight. If we were separate from it, it would seem*

lovely. We would breathe in delight seeing it in a movie. [but we can't watch as if uninvolved]

The machine is, of course, a centrifuge. [Donne again updated, with this flung-outwardness of physical separation associated with uranium, fissionable material, the bomb, our half-lives] *We're locked* [back to this word, specifying their prison as the whirling earth] *on its outside walls by the magnetic soles of our feet,* [like a carnival ride, but also gravity rooting them to their separated spots, frustrating (and sustaining?) their love] *the veins branching downwards.* [I'm lost, but maybe the veins – blood, leaf – holding us to the earth] *I think of a glass anatomical model of a man, with an erection.* [shocks: trans. The test tube sticking out?]

As if the earth had gone transparent and its gross axis become visible, turning us. [OK, with revolving world and sexual force of life joined by "gross"] *Like a drill-core spectrum, a blackened rainbow,* [wow! an imaginative coup to find this comparison, the lost brightness still visible; images shifting so fast now, sentence by sentence, without losing vividness and exactness] *the red orange yellow at the centre* [rushing with no commas as if our whirling through space has accelerated] *further towards the ends* [possessive?] *roughness, jumble, glisten of coal* [rephrases "a rubble of dark and rough and glitter"] *and oil pools, moving capillaries* [set up by "veins branching downward"] *of water.* [what sustains us] *The ends themselves hard glossy white, ice that never melts.* [caps, poles, the endless coldness and hardness that bereaves us]. *The effortless spin* [of earth, and Fate's web] *of the thing generating so much brute power.* [like a turbine, clarifying the earlier use of "brute"]

Sometimes I think I can see you across the curvature of the walls. [in imagery an echo of Hamlet: world as prison]. *We might reach out, try to touch.*

But the machine holds us motionless. Our muscles flatten, our veins and arteries spread out like maps. [like roads to each other that can't be travelled] *We are splayed, pinned down on separate beds, in separate cities.*

I'm turning downward into sleep. I will not dream of you. [seeming rejection] *Slowly, slowly, it's turning you towards your morning.* [someone further east is waking, but is there also a prescient pun on "mourning," or is it just a misreading, a retroactive significance given by the newspaper on my desk: "BODY IDENTITY CONFIRMED"?] *You are beginning to remember me.* [the beloved will replicate her awakening, begin the poem again, reciprocally, from his consciousness of her?]

I'd like to read "The Face" at a memorial service, but it might stun the family to hear this remarkable love letter. I'll phone Fred to see if a gathering has already been organized.

Outside, on the trees and bushes and wet grass, there's no natural light left. Just a yellowish glare of human making. "She had apparently been killed by a head blow which fractured her skull." No answer.

I'll try Moira once more. The paper said she had at least two children. "Always when I wake. . . . " Her voice had a freshness no creative writing instructor could teach. Nobody's answering. Moira, you bitch! My Galatea who refuses to be sculpted. By these hands anyway.

The last time I heard Willie's voice on the phone it had a restlessness I had to recognize as my own. Though our languages differ, we have the same sense of Romantic performance. Two suburban outlaws. Why would he take a triangular ruler? It makes no sense. I wasn't content to sleep only with my wife forever, and disappeared from my Vancouver home. Jane, I'm sorry. Who knows how to keep a heart from nodding off?

Her murder will become part of a mystique now, that will mix image and achievement confusingly. Alternatively, Pat's death might mean a lessening of reputation because all her potential books will be coldly subtracted, and the poems already written might disappear entirely in lurid talk and the reverent hush of her biography. Neglect would be a second silencing of this woman who could compose the precise emotive details of our lives into the music of words with an aching clarity – that's an expression I should remember, maybe for her funeral. Her lyrics so lovely, so like a rock-slide.

Open like the mouth of the shark in *Jaws*. The story of my life still open. Un-fated, un-Moira-fied?

It's hard to imagine Willie's motives. "A triangular affair"?

I get out a blank examination booklet, and begin to write:

Today I swiped one of those triangular rulers – not those clear flat ones made outta plastic we're suppose to get for geometry class, but one of those three-sided things.

What a drag, man, back for another whole YEAR of boredom. I nearly nodded off in the first math class, with the four-eyed teach going on about alge-BRA. Didja see that new chick Sonya who thinks she's so cool, and her tits are like two fried eggs?

Mom keeps nagging me about how high school can be a new start for me. Yeah, right. What an airhead. She had this brainstorm I can wear Uncle Bob's pajamas because they were never used, and he was a nice clean man who always liked me. The buttons look like slices from a yucky banana. Mom stuffs them into my bottom drawer, like I'm gonna sleep in some stiff's threads!

Anyways, I'm in the drugstore after school, figuring to score some safes, and the witch by the cash register in a pink nurse's uniform is eyeballing me. I move to an aisle further away and pretend like I'm real interested in EN-VELOPES, checking out all the different sizes and prices and those air mail ones for faraway places, when I spot one of those rulers. Two sides I can understand, one for inches and the other for that metric shit, but three? It had all those different markings and scales that mean nothing.

I can see it won't fit in my pocket. But I grab one quick and shove it up my shirt, where it looks like King Kong's pecker. And I'm outta the door and on the sidewalk before I hear her voice: "That's shop-lifting, son." I don't know why I waited like a zombie to be caught.

At least my old man isn't around anymore to play the heavy, and mess with my head. I shoulda boosted a motorcycle instead of that nerdy ruler.

But, Hey! I could lift the keys to Mom's Rabbit. Whatta-ya-say, man? A couple days on the road and we could be catching some rays in California. Some monster waves rolling in like blue glass, the white foam on top like some far-out drink, the rush of it all, riding to the rescue of some surfer chicks

"Measures." Would that be a workable title?

I'd better phone Jane.

Willie's baby face, so new and soft and without guile: maskless. His eyes never suspected that the looks of love on his parents' faces were removable.

Tofino, BC
August 26, 1997

Dear Keith,
Thanks for sending the copies of your first chapter. It was very interesting, though over my head I think! I don't know if you want comments. I was wondering if you'd please consider using recycled and non-chlorine bleached paper, and using both sides of the page.
Roy was 52, not 42.
I know you're just trying to portray a character, but I hate, repeat Hate! the "tits" comment.
I love the last line. It resonates with me a lot as you no doubt can imagine!
My partner and I hiked all over Hornby in July. I hadn't been there for 15 years. Loved it. Great place, so different from Tofino!

Sincerely Chris L

Vancouver
Sept. 9th 1998

Dear Keith:
At long last. Forgive me not writing with my comments sooner as I've been preoccupied with my grandmother's death in May, & becoming that sociologist's conundrum, the "single mom." Also, Chris Weisenthal from U. of Alberta recently made her pilgrimage to see our infamous cardboard boxes. She's interested in writing a cultural biography. Her CV's quite impressive, & she brought roses!

As to your work in progress, of course it's lovely (I'm not worthy! She cried) & I'm not concerned with the impure thoughts of its characters. I'd be more concerned if they had none – how boring! My misgivings. I was perfectly comfortable with the gentle, improvisational "field notes" applied to critical theory with "Notes on Notes." I was initially somewhat nervous, however, after reading "Black Rainbows." After some thought, I felt it must be the potential, good or bad, of what seems essentially a new genre that was bothering me, i.e., what happens when a murdered woman's body of work is taken up in this way into a living man's larger body of work, & in the lives and minds of his characters? Done well & lovingly: a synthesis, a rebirth, a celebration. Done insensitively, what? A tampering with the remains, or worse, dismemberment? Yikes! It has to be done so carefully. You can see one of the reasons why I've taken so long to respond has been my trying to make sense of my thoughts & the struggle to be clear, etc.

The good news is: I trust you to do it well and lovingly. I've been fond of the folks you've created so far. They seem warm & human to me, even the bastards. Just please make sure that while Professor Williams mentally ruminates over Moira's breasts (& who among us has not done the same? Let he/she cast the first Wonderbra!) he & his colleagues take good care of my mommy.

Sincerely & with best wishes
Beth Lowther

P.S. Please call or write if you've any questions. My best to JoAnn (whom Zsuzsi Gartner described as "so cool"), & to your sons.

The Chinese Greengrocers

They live their days in a fragrance
of white and black grapes
and tomatoes and the fresh
water smell of lettuce.

They know with their hands
and noses the value
of all things grown.
They will make you a bargain price
on overripe cantaloupe.

They wash with clear water
their bunches of carrots
and radishes. They crank out
a canvas awning to shelter them.

Their babies suckle on unsold bananas.
By the age of six
they can all make change
and tell which fruits are ripe.

The grandmothers know only numbers
in English, and the names
of fruits and vegetables.

They open before the supermarkets open,
they are open all day,
they eat with an eye on the door.

They keep sharp eyes
for shoplifting children.
They know every customer's
brand of cigarettes.

After the neighbourhood movies are out
and the drugstores have all closed
they bring in their blueberries
and cabbages and potted flowers.

In the rooms behind the store
they speak in their own language.
Their speech flies around the rooms
like swooping, pecking birds.
Far into the night I believe
they weigh balsa baskets
of plums, count ears of corn
and green peppers

No matter how they may wash
their fingers, their very pores
are perfumed with green,
and they sleep with parsley and peaches
onions and oranges
and grapes and running water.

• Pat Lowther

Sunday morning, October 19, 1975

From the doorway I notice a large glass tank with crabs crawling over each other's backs. Then, in the far corner at a round table, my gel-haired brother, who stands up quickly.

"Emily."

"Hi, Paul."

His lips touch my cheeks quickly, as our bodies brush. He moves away so fast I'm left staring at a red and gold banner with thick black Chinese characters, which probably mean "Good Fortune." Paul yanks out a chair for me with an efficient dentist's hand, his professional voice asking, "How's work?"

"OK, I guess, Paul. A friend of mine was murdered."

Paul snaps the wooden head of his chopsticks in two. "I'm sorry. News like that brings back the day when Shirley walked into my office with a squished tadpole on her sweater."

How could I have expected empathy? His own story

still too compelling, too close, and women are supposed to be good listeners.

A waiter pushes a three-tiered trolley shaped like a wedding cake at us. Steamed shrimp dumplings, sticky rice balls, crisp fried noodles, squid, and scallops with snow peas. Already a second trolley is coming, with soups and spring rolls and mysterious things I can't give a name to. When I gesture at the dumplings, the waiter squeezes them in shiny tongs and sets them down delicately on my plate. I unwrap my chopsticks, and crack them apart.

Paul, chewing and gulping, signals the waiter for more food to be shifted onto his crowded plate. Always, his appetite has dwarfed mine. Out the window, still a grey morning.

"Emily, aren't you going to try the squid?"

Shallow knife-slits have been made cross-ways on the pieces of its body, to form a raised diamond pattern when they cook. Their tiny tentacles, abandoned on top, look like severed hands. "No thanks." I listen, as a server speaks in his own language to a Chinese couple near the papered wall, hear a kind of faraway singing in my ears, and his repeated sound, "Hie, hie." Yes?

"Pass the soya sauce, Em."

Maybe Paul and I can talk about the weather. "A couple of days ago, it looked like Vancouver would be washed out into the Pacific Ocean."

"Haven't you heard that B.C. is God's country, Emily? There's a desert in Chile where it hasn't rained for a thousand years. Would you rather live there?"

"I don't want to be glum."

"Paradise is not in the atlas, Emily. Here's round three of the trolleys. Would you like another dumpling? In Hawaii, there's a mountain top where it rains every day."

"I don't really have an appetite for all these goodies."

"That's why you are a Leftist social worker. But don't worry, the NDP will lose the next election and you'll no longer have a chance to feel privileged. Nothing but steamed rice for you."

"The Socreds are going to be steamed after we beat them again." When I pick up my two chopsticks, I'm reminded of Olga's story. "Paul, did you hear about a Chinese man who visited both heaven and hell?"

My kid brother glances at me for a split second: his teeth pause. His skin has an old person's sheen now, like the translucent pastry on the dumplings.

I start to tell him, "This man visited hell and found people sitting around a table pretty much like this one, its huge round top covered with delicious food on a red tablecloth, but everyone looked miserable. Then he noticed they all had to use yard-long chopsticks to reach their food."

"Shouldn't this story be in metres?"

"By any measurement, they were very unhappy at this feast. Tormented, in fact, because if someone managed to pick up a tantalizing dumpling, say, with the long wooden implements, as she or he bent the arm towards the mouth, the tasty morsel would end up behind the neck, or if he or she clumsily tried to shorten the grip, on the floor. So the visitor hurried to heaven, where to his astonishment it was exactly the same! People seated at a feast clutched yard-long chopsticks, but now everyone was smiling. Why?"

"I'm swallowing."

"How can Shirley live with you? Why?"

"I don't know the answer to your riddle. They were on uppers?"

"They weren't feeding themselves."

"How? I don't get it."

"In heaven, the portions they picked up with their long chopsticks were fed to the person across the table."

"They were feeding each other? It sounds like a fable from Chairman Mao."

"Or Christ." This outing for dim sum was supposed to be fun, but I'm just getting pissed off at Paul.

"I don't want some stranger jamming sticks down my throat, and feeding me stuff I don't want."

"That's what your patients get."

"I don't need some uncoordinated person jabbing tofu in my ear."

"It would serve you right, Paul. It's been my experience that dentists like to talk, especially when a patient has an electric drill whining in her frozen mouth, next to a slurping suction hose, and is wearing a suffocating rubber dam."

A smile twitches on his face as he seizes some more fried noodles.

"Paul, in that Chinese heaven, you might actually have to listen for a change. How does Shirley put up with you?"

"She says to say hello, and is fine. But you haven't tasted a biteful, Em. Here." His chopsticks waver like tentacles in front of my eyes, before he picks a dumpling off my plate. Paul dips it in soya sauce, and directs it towards my teeth.

I open my mouth and bite through the slippery skin, tasting salt flavours on my tongue. Swallow and feel better. Again, Paulie lifts his chopsticks, and I mouth the shiny morsel held between the tight wooden tips. Shredding and crunching the dumpling, before letting it slide down inside me. "Thanks."

"Did I ever tell you how Shirley ran into my office that day?"

At least four times.

"I was just about to put in a temporary crown for a patient, when I turned around to see a tadpole smeared onto my wife's sweater. Her face was patched with mud. The poor patient, Mrs. Humphreys, had gone rigid, but then leaped out of the chair, still wearing the bib."

After adjusting the positioning of my fingers, I grab at a sticky rice ball.

"The pain in Shirley's voice – " He puts down his handle-less cup of tea without drinking from it.

Paul's wife is the last person in the world I can imagine wearing a dead tadpole. But she found herself in a place where smart clothes, manicured hands, elegantly coiffed hair meant nothing.

"Shirley jerked me outside, where her car's front wheels were parked in the flower bed. On the passenger seat, a small muddy running shoe. One of Lucy's."

Paulie scoops up his porcelain cup and drains the tea. "That was six months ago." He pinches at a piece of crab left on his once-heaped plate, then lays aside his chopsticks without eating. "I was still holding the crown between my thumb and index finger."

"How are you and Shirley doing now?"

He doesn't even peek at the dessert trolley, just-arrived, with sweets and fruits. I wave away the smiling waiter.

"For the longest day of our lives we both believed Lucy had drowned in that pond out in back of our place. In a slough of despond, Em. When it turned out to be an abduction – and the police brought our little daughter back – it was like a prayer had been answered. Shirley takes her religion very, very seriously now. And who am I to argue, with Lucy returned to us, alive and well? Both of them are at church right now."

He bows his head down, over his nearly empty plate.

"I know I've already told you this, but when the police brought her back early the next morning, in bare feet and a blanket, they kept saying she was 'unharmed.' But all the airiness had leaked out of Shirley and me. Whenever Lucy, nimble and careless, jumps over a log at the beach, we run to catch her."

He looks across the round table at me, his eyes blinking wetly. Paul has always been afraid of his tears. I cover his small hand with mine. "I'm the social worker." A financial aid worker with a staggering case load never quite typed up and filed away. Too many teary, boozy, gentle, cursing, lovely people needing new eyeglasses, better medication, some food, a pair of waterproof shoes, a bit of luck before the next welfare cheque.

"I nearly lost my daughter, Em, and ended up losing my wife. We're still married, but Shirley's been born again. I'm in kind of a dead zone. Everything's frozen, but the nerve endings jangle. But tell me about your life. I'm worried about my big sis. Why did that awful thing happen to your friend?"

"I don't know." Because Pat was a woman? "Jealousy was probably a factor."

"That crazy woman who snatched Lucy just wanted to be a mother."

"Pat Lowther left behind two kids. A big gap. She was a very fine poet, an activist, and my friend." On the red linen tablecloth, my hand is a fist. Paulie places his hand over mine. "Some weeks back, her husband advised me that she had deserted him and his family. Two days ago the police identified her body."

The smiling waiter circles our table twice, bows his head a few inches, and leaves us the bill in an ugly-brown plastic tray.

My brother leans forward to read the total, then drops his credit card on top.

"No, I can't let you. We'll split it."

"My treat, Em," he says. "I'll be back in a moment."

After the break-up with Julio, I stopped eating, hoping I might just float away. No physical sign Julio had entered another person's body, so what was the harm? But I couldn't get rid of a sense of heaviness, sinking me down, nearly all the way to China.

I get up from the round table. A large crab, being lifted out of the glass tank, squeezes its claw at the innocent air. Outside, water is still hitting the sidewalk.

My brother strides towards me, with the brisk pace of someone who has a patient waiting in the next room.

"Thanks."

Under the fluorescent light Paulie opens his arms wide and hugs me. Silently, we wish each other better fortune. He hugs me so close and long that I feel be-loved again.

Anemones

Under the wharf at Saturna
the sea anemones
open their velvet bodies

chalk black
   and apricot
      and lemon-white

they grow as huge
and glimmering
     as flesh chandeliers

under the warped
and salt-stained wharf
   letting down
      their translucent mouths
              of arms

even the black ones
have an aura
like an afterimage of light

Under our feet
   the gorgeous animals
     are feeding
         in the sky

• Pat Lowther

Tuesday, October 21, 1975

This island again.

I lean on the open door of our unmarked car, see the grey sand reaching out from the two sides of the ferry dock, like tired arms.

The high pilings are exposed by the low tide – tall black creosote posts capped by shiny aluminium to keep the rain water out. The tops of the poles that jut into the air and the lower parts that hide in the ocean bed last longer than the dozen or so feet of wood in between, which become wet and dry as the tide rises and falls away. Where air and water go back and forth, enclosing the wood in turns, rot happens the fastest.

We slide in between the high bulwarks. Mayne Island. The metal ramp bangs down on the ship's deck, angling up sharply to Village Bay.

"John Jorgensen?"

I see a puffy face with fuzzy ears, beneath an officer's white peaked cap. Gold braid on a navy-blue uniform. "Yes?"

"Curly Jones."

All at once I am looking at this round ferry captain, trying to find the boy inside. The one who flew us into the night skies over Germany in a Halifax bomber, and got us all back home to County Durham. Moose Squadron, Number 419. Bald now, so curly only in a manner of speaking. "Still in uniform, I see. I used to wear one with the Vancouver police."

"Getting the gen on criminals, eh, Johnny? It must be a bit like navigating."

"Well, you try not to get lost."

"Did you notice we nearly had to throw the engines into reverse off Georgina Point? Some guy in a rowboat had hooked a big salmon in Active Pass, and no ferry whistle was going to make him get out of our way. Oh, I saw Sparks a few months ago. He's now some high mucky-muck with B.C. Hydro. A Vice-President of something."

"I haven't seen any of the crew in years. But I'm still married to the woman I met overseas. We've two grown-up sons who're doing well, and a daughter in school." *Is there anything you wish to tell me?*

"Tom, my only child, went across the border and enlisted in the U.S. Air Force. He was helicoptered out in April, with nearly the last of the American troops in South Vietnam."

Cars are starting to unload.

"Well, Curly, maybe there's a chance for change now, with things like that joint US-Soviet space mission. It's pretty amazing to see the Apollo spacecraft dock with the Soviet Soyuz. It has to be important for those guys to come together, and look down on the same earth."

"Those Commies will never give up, Johnny, not until they rule the whole world. And getting control of the high ground of outer space is how you do it. It just makes good military sense."

A bitter Cold Warrior. "You may be right, Curly."

"It's global combat."

I hear our car engine start, as the line ahead begins to move. "Good seeing you again, Curly. I'd better go." My partner's big hands on the steering wheel. I get in the ghost car, roll down the window. Even if the Russian probes have just given us the first pictures from the surface of Venus, we're far from finding love.

"Say hi to Lynn for me."

"You bet." Surprised he remembered her name. But now recall we were on leave together in London when I first met her. Lynn's hair outside her pale raincoat, a black and shiny tangle under the lamp glare.

My partner glances across at me as he drives us onto Mayne Island.

"That was an old Air Force buddy from Bomber Command. Our Captain."

"He seems pretty gung-ho."

"You've got to remember, Alex, nearly ten thousand Canadian airmen were lost."

This morning Lynn had red eyelids, her whole face ugly from suffering. "John, before you go, I need to show you something in Ursula's room."

She pointed with her eyes through the open door. I peered in at a teenager's mess: an unmade bed, pulled-out drawers, clothes on the floor scattered inside-out. Like a crime site. All around us, strange faces pouted and snarled from posters and album covers.

Lynn stepped over a balled-up blue shirt, and picked up the cat-shaped teapot with tiny flowers printed on it, a long-ago Christmas gift from Aunt Mary in Czechoslovakia. Its spout, a white paw. She lifted off the lid, and pulled out a small plastic baggie with a red twist tie. Mary, Jesus, and Joseph. In my own house. I almost didn't recognize it. Even before opening it, I could breath in the musky spice of marijuana. Yellowish green, and probably enough for eight joints. At the bottom of the teapot – "tea pot," her joke? – an evil fat joint bulging out the twisted white paper.

I could have killed someone. Lynn had her hands pressed against the top of her head, like a prisoner of war who had just surrendered. Out of habit, I started searching the drawers. In the top one, behind some underwear and socks, I found the silver cross Ursula no longer wears around her neck. Then, behind the mirror, her diary, stuffed with newspaper clippings. I wish I hadn't.

Once our sweet little girl. Now totally out of control.

"John, what are we going to do?"

"I don't know. Alex has been waiting outside for ten minutes now, and we've got a ferry to catch. I'll have to call you later."

A cop with a criminal for a daughter, but I didn't tell Curly that, or even my partner.

Mayne Island. There is the hotel and our other vehicle.

"Everything okay back home, Johnny?"

"Right as rain, Alex."

"I can put the children in the hands of the Human Resource people, and phone you when the time comes. I'll drop you off here."

"Fine, Alex. Thanks." Great. Except I've just started reading my daughter's diary, and discovered she is doing drugs, has become fixated on Patty Hearst, is experimenting with sex. "I'll review the notes, and begin the paperwork."

I get out of the unmarked car, and pull her small, clasped book from my jacket pocket.

A blotter of acid he had tucked inside his panama hat and afterwards we went tripping through the streets gronking on uptight faces and far-out dogs and laughing at the way lines of blood moved through our skinless see-through arms and the only bring-down was looking for new albums and hearing soft-rock shit by Poco and Loggins and Messina

Just taking a trip. A sortie.

Lynn said she was going to seek guidance from Father Marinelli.

"A reservation for Sergeants Jorgensen and Ezzy. One night. Two singles."

"Yes, Sir. Just sign here, please. Here's your key. The room's just at the top of the stairs."

Why would she collect news items when she doesn't

even do her homework? I'll review the documents up there. How can I be exhausted from sitting on my butt for four straight hours? I drop the suitcase, and turn the key. I open the door, go into a small cool room meant for strangers.

> **Patty was "held in closet" Patty lived in a "fantasy world"** When the blindfold was removed, "she felt as if she were on some LSD trip. Everything was out of proportion," big and distorted.

As a tiny kid, Ursula threw herself into a pool, believing she could swim, and nearly drowned. She went down, kicking and thrashing. For years after she was rescued she wouldn't go near water.

> Meanwhile, after each meal all sorts of fantastic shapes and images kept coming and going before her eyes, so that the faces of the kidnappers and jailers appeared to her as weird and horrible masks. . . .

Really just this skinny boy with peach fuzz on his upper lip who blushes all the time but he wanted me to skip school again so we could go see that dumb flick Jaws and laugh at all the people in the Vogue shivering at make-believe horrors but I think he secretly just wanted a cheap thrill safe in a plush seat eating hot-buttered popcorn and slurping my drink but he does come up with these far out phrases like

*"terror bingeing" and "a visual laxative" that
allows "dread to be shat out for a few hours"*

A real smart-ass jerk loser bastard she's met up with. Inside that poster's circle shape, the nearly naked shape of a swimmer: womanly and girlish. Huge waiting teeth. Is she "terror binging"?

To continue flying you had to be oblivious to what was lurking below. Only a thin aluminium shell kept the sky out, and it was useless against shrapnel.

Years after she nearly drowned, we drove out to the beach at Spanish Banks. The tide was coming in, over perfect shell-like ridges of hard brown sand. I was throwing a rubber football with the boys and noticed Ursula laying herself down on her back in the shallow sea-water. Her young legs sank a bit, but then she was floating all by herself on the salty dark-green water. Rocking gently with the waves, slowly drifting out into Burrard Inlet, headed towards the freighters from the Orient. She kept smiling at her bobbing, sunlit toes, as Lynn and I squinted into the midday glare at our blissful daughter moving effortlessly, on top of the watery world.

My one conversation with her in weeks, a sour failure.

("Ursula, the French teacher reports she hasn't seen you for a month, un mois."

"The class is a drag, and boring with a capital 'B.' I'm dropping it."

"What about all those French painters you used to love?"

"They didn't need words."

"You need to take a language to graduate."

"I don't care."

"Is there anything you wish to tell me?"

"No."

"Until you get a passing grade in French, you're grounded."

"You're … a *cochon*.")

I can't stop reading the diary I stole:

> *Dennis so eager and boyish at first not even*
> *waiting to get to my bedroom and not knowing*
> *what to do after his purple shirt with black*
> *stars was thrown on the rug and his panama*
> *hat had bumped off and the pillow with hard*
> *buttons pressed against the side of my face*

I can't read this.

> *and the pillow with hard buttons pressed*
> *against the side of my face while I lay back on*
> *the scratchy chesterfield*

I'd arrest her boyfriend if I could. She'd never look at me with love again.

> *his hot breath coming through all the long hair*
> *covering his face like some black sheepdog and*
> *only his teeth showed as he rubbed and slipped*
> *down there while my coolest tape of the Stones*
> *was jumping and beating and shouting so right*
> *that it was like Jumping Jack Flash had*
> *strutted right inside my head flashing and*
> *dancing away all the dead-eyed world*

142

To put a stop to. Arrest. Probably from the French, arreter, which likely has some kind of accent on it. Funny to *stop* and think of that connection after all those years. Madame Framboise. Mrs. Raspberry, we called her. To impede, delay, detain. To put a stop to, too late.

Before the war I wanted to become an astronomer

Felt so good but dumb Dennis probably doesn't even know I've got a clit and I was going to come – interesting way to describe the leaving and arriving that's orgasm – his sneaky skinny body on top sliding on the outside of me when I began to shudder deliciously shouting my breath away

Graphic stuff, and stomach-wrenching if it's written by your fifteen-year old daughter. Like swallowing down a whole bottle of thick poison.

I'm almost out of breath, from just bending over to pick up a clipping that has floated out of her diary. Part of me wishes to be fifteen again?

. . . instructed by them that she must accompany them to the bank, that she must allow herself to be photographed by the bank camera. And, in addition, she was told she must announce her name aloud so that everyone would know she was participating in the holdup.

The document said that about three to four days after her release from the closet, Miss

Hearst was put into a car and
driven to a branch of the
Hibernia Bank in San Francisco
and was "given a gun and di-
rected to stand about in the centre of the bank counter."

Meanwhile, one of her cap-
tors, armed with a gun which
was kept pointed at her, kept an
eye on her and had told her in
advance that if she made one
false move or did anything except announce her name, she
would be killed immediately, the
affidavit said.

I have to phone Lynn. It's like suddenly discover-
ing the fourteenth moon of Jupiter, which must have
been there all the time. Never noticed it before in its
remote orbit. But this toxic stuff is where we live: our
only daughter.

*for one long minute I'm happy as happy even
when he sprays burning glop on my belly*

There's stuff here I can't be alone with anymore.
I'll wait in the lobby for the call from Alex.

*After I'm lying there awhile like a cooling
corpse I want to slash both my wrists and wear
my sleeves up to show the world*

I throw the diary into the top drawer, next to the
Gideon Bible, and grab the keys to the other car. I stumble going down the steps, almost sprawl into the lobby.
As parents we did nothing wrong. God knows, we tried
with all our might.

An old man with rheumy eyes looks up from his muddy shoes, moves his mouth sideways a few times, asks, "Are you a visitor here?"

"Yes."

"Fewer than five hundred people live on Mayne Island year round, so I suspected you were a stranger. But more than a hundred years ago, during the Gold Rush, thousands of men used to stop off here because it was halfway between Vancouver Island and the Mainland. Most of them stayed at a place that's now called Miners Bay. Then they rowed on across the Gulf, all the way to the mouth of the Fraser River to pan for nuggets. Their fortune."

"Sergeant, the call is for you."

"Thanks. Hello."

"Johnny, the children have been placed on the boat. I am now following his car as it is heading in the direction of the cabin at Sleepy Hollow."

"Okay, Alex. I'll proceed."

"Say, are you some kind of policeman?"

"Yes. I'm on duty now."

Grateful for action, I hurry out to the parking lot, and unlock the car door. I jump in, start the car, and accelerate out on a cold engine. Turning onto the main road I try to drive without thinking about Ursula. A dense, invisible presence beside me. No way to protect our daughter, when even the sky is falling: scientists now saying the freons in spray cans and fridges are destroying the atmosphere, so we'll all die of skin cancer.

Perhaps.

Not many miles on this island. I pop the flashing light up, and there he is, followed by Alex. I flick on the siren for a few seconds, and block the suspect's vehicle. The man stops his car, and I park to the side of the road, close to the ditch. I step out with my hand on the holster.

When he gets out, I stand directly in front of him.

"Roy Lowther, I am Detective-Sergeant Jorgensen. We are investigating the death of your wife, Patricia Lowther. There is evidence to show she was murdered and I believe you are responsible. As a result, I'm arresting you, for homicide." His strong face teary. My watch says 4:13 p.m. I motion him towards the other side of his car, where Alex holds the passenger door open.

I get in the driver's side of his vehicle. We start down the narrow country road with my partner tailing us.

"It is my duty to warn you that you are not obliged to say anything, but anything you do say may be given in evidence."

"You have taken my children. I have nothing to say."

"Would you like to phone your lawyer?"

"In your presence?"

"Yes, I'm afraid so. I've found blood on the hammer I took from you. Do you have an explanation?"

"No explanation. You have taken my children. I have no heart."

"Your children will be looked after well."

Not even by rich parents like the Hearts. Their daughter, a heroine of sorts to Ursula. Imagines herself to be fighting evil, flying through flak-filled skies.

Risking everything to make the world right. Nearly shot down twice.

I have no heart.

I want to take those two little, parentless daughters home to Lynn, and start over.

Slugs

Yellow gray
      boneless things
  live like phlegm
heaving themselves
gracelessly
across sidewalks

laboured
as though the earth
were not their element
oozing their viscid mess
  for godsake don't
         step
             there

ugh ugh
horrible pulp

:two of them:
the slime from their bodies
makes a crystal rope
     suspending
them   in air
    under
  the apple tree

  they are twined
    together

in a perfect spiral
   flowing
          around
   each other
       spinning
   gently
      with their motions
Imagine
   making love like that

• Pat Lowther

Tuesday, April 6, 1976

> Q *Perhaps – excuse me, could you just
> slow down a bit because people are
> trying to take notes, okay?*

hustling to keep up with the rush of words

> Q *When did you meet Pat Lowther?*
>
> A *It was in 1972 in October.*
>
> Q *Was that in Vancouver?*
>
> A *Yes, it was in Vancouver.*
>
> Q *And your present occupation, Sir?*
>
> A *I'm a university professor.*

love these seconds of silence as the judge finishes writing down his notes

> Q *And on that trip to Vancouver were you
> giving a poetry reading at UBC?*

A   Yes, I read at UBC. and also at the
    Vancouver Art Gallery.

like a brief holiday

Q   And did you have lunch with Pat
    Lowther on that occasion?

A   Yes, Pat came to the reading at the art
    gallery and I invited her out for lunch
    the next day.

my boyfriend hardly ever talks

Q   Did you meet with her again the same
    year in Edmonton at a conference?

A   Yes, I did.

Q   And following that, did you meet again
    at another conference?

A   Yes.

touches the release and lifts the hood

Q   And were these conferences spaced far
    in time?

A   Yes, the – the – let me see, the 1972
    conference was in Edmonton and then
    the 19 – the 1973, I saw her in Victoria,
    and then again in 1974 in Fredericton,
    New Brunswick.

Q   How did you regard her poetry?

A   Very highly. I admired it a great deal.

Doug bending over in the sunshine the black t-shirt
riding up his bare back pale smooth skin except for
shiny pairs of knuckles curving along his spinal cord

> Q   Did you correspond with Pat Lowther
> during this period of time?

> A   Yes, I did. I began corresponding with
> her before that in – I think in the late
> sixties. W e printed some of her poetry
> in the late sixties. And in 1970 I was on
> sabbatical leave and living in England
> and I wrote to her from England asking
> for a copy of her first book, "This
> Difficult Flowering," which she sent to
> me. Also, last year I was supposed to
> give a paper at the Northeast Modern
> Language Association meeting in
> Montreal and I was going to give a
> paper on her poetry. Unfortunately, I
> was snowed in and I never gave the
> paper.

get into this mind space where I can flick shorthand
words onto the paper

> Q   Now, on September 12th, 1975 in Wind-
> sor did you receive a telephone call?

> A   Yes, I did.

> Q   And as a result of this telephone call,
> did you embark upon a course of con-
> duct?

tuning up

A   Yes, I wrote a letter to Pat the same day.

Q   Now, to explain, please, what you did as
     a result of the telephone call, would
     you tell us what the telephone call
     consisted of?

his chrome tools match the sheen of new spark plugs

A   The caller, first of all, asked me my
     name. He said, "I'm calling from To-
     ronto."

THE COURT: Just pausing there. Mr.
     Doust, is this something that you take
     exception to – to hearing?

MR. DOUST: I take no exception at this
     point, Your Honour.

THE COURT: All right.

afraid might look down and see my boyfriend's name
typed in "Doug" wiping away the grease or impolite
words about the judge who sits on high trying to look
dignified blowing his nose

Q   I'm sorry, the caller gave a name?

in front of others pretending

A   The caller warned me against coming
     to the League of Canadian Poets meet-
     ing, which was to be held in Victoria in
     October, and he told me that if I did
     come to the meeting, that my wife and
     children would have to find out what
     my real reason for going was, what my
     sleeping arrangements were to be. Then

153

he hung up.

Doug's square head peering down and his tight butt in tight jeans and heavy Kodiak boots lifting at the heels

> THE COURT: *I'm sorry, you're going to have to go over the last part, that if you did come, that your wife and children would know the real reason?*
>
> A   *Yes, but he didn't elaborate on that.*

never says a word as he tightens with a satisfying snick

> Q   *Well, you did say something after using the words "your real reason." What was said?*
>
> A   *He said what my sleeping arrangements would be. Then he also said, "Make some excuse to the chairwoman. Do not go."*
>
> Q   *The chairwoman?*

the witness means Pat Lowther

> A   *Chairwoman. And then he – then he hung up.*

but he gives me a chance to find my own words after days of hearing strangers'

> Q   *Now, you say that you wrote a letter to Pat Lowther in relation to that telephone call?*
>
> A   *Yes, I did.*

Q   *And did you mail it?*

A   *Yes, I did.*

a putting into running order no movement wasted

Q   *I've shown to counsel what is a sealed*
envelope and I'm opening the envelope
to produce the contents. It's an envelope
with a Manila tag attached that is
unsealed with some writing on the tag,
writing on the back, and some initials
in the top right corner.

the trick to get him to pause tilt his head across the
engine my way

There is inside a white envelope with
typing on it, and some letterhead on
the envelope itself.

by weighing in the palm of my hand the blackened
sparkplug he's just taken out can get him to consider
what I'm saying

It's date stamped, 12th day, 9th month,
1975, "Windsor, Ontario," addressed to
Pat Lowther. And inside producing on a
blank sheet of white paper – it has
some initials on the back for the record
– dated September 12th, 1975, at the
bottom of the typing there is the words,
"love, Gene," is that correct?

A   *Yes.*

Q   *Is that your writing?*

> A   Yes, it is.

listens to my words like testimony

> Q   Would you examine that, Sir, and tell
>   the Court if that's the letter you wrote
>   —
>
> A   Yes, this —
>
> Q   — in response to the telephone call?

my fingers needing to fly to catch two voices speaking
at once

> A   This is the letter that I wrote to Pat in
>   response to that phone call.
>
> MR. DEBOU: I'd ask, Your Honour, that
>   everything that I've described be
>   marked as one exhibit in these proceed-
>   ings, the envelope and its contents.
>
> THE COURT: Exhibit Z are we at?
>
> MR. DEBOU: Yes, Your Honour.
>
> THE COURT: Exhibit Z, all right.
>
> (Letter to Pat Lowther, and accompanying
> envelopes, etcetera, marked Exhibit Z.)

don't begrudge Doug the Corvette he loves so dearly
but twice he has nearly killed us on the Squamish highway once cornering too fast shaking and hugging me
after black ice

> Q   Did you receive any written communi-

cation from Pat Lowther in response to that letter?

A   *Yes, I did.*

the second time not really his fault due to the other driver crossing the line

Q   *And did you have any telephone conversation with Pat Lowther in relation to that?*

A   *Yes, I did. In her letter she said that she would call me on the afternoon of September 19th from her office at UBC, which she did do.*

Q   *And was that on September 19th, 1975 that she telephoned you?*

A   *Yes. Yes, it was.*

Q   *And did you discuss this letter that – or, I'm sorry, the telephone call that you had received?*

A   *Yes, we did.*

THE COURT: *I'm sorry, the date again that you talked –*

A   *September 19th.*

THE COURT: *Thank you. All right. Let me see the letter. Go ahead.*

Q   *And after your conversation with Pat Lowther on September 19th, were you*

still intending on going to the confer-
ence over the Thanksgiving weekend in
October, 1975 in Victoria?

A   I hadn't made up my mind. I was still
in doubt.

the problem in persuading Doug to marry me may be
how to get him to believe it's his idea

Q   And did you communicate to Pat
Lowther whether you would be coming
or not to that conference in that tel-
ephone call?

A   No, I told her I hadn't made up my
mind.

Q   In any of this correspondence that you
had between Pat Lowther and yourself,
were there any references to "Brain
Damage"?

A   Yes, there were.

pimples and ears that stick out I'm not as cute as my
sister

Q   Can you explain that, Sir?

A   I don't remember the year but Pat
wrote to me to tell me that she had
been receiving flowers from a young
musician who was playing in a rock
music group called Brain Damage, and
I think she was making a joke of it,
receiving the flowers and the attention

*from the young man, and asked my
advice. And in the same spirit I wrote a
rather jocular note saying, "Tell him
that he'll have to – that I understand
his feelings but he'll just have to tough
it out."*

Q   *Are you familiar with the book, "Diving for the Body"?*

A   *Yes, I am. I wrote it.*

his body lying on the pavement by those hubcaps with
crossed flags and when I kneeled down to see what he
was doing so long on his back under a ton of bright
red curves he dropped his wrench

Q   *I've shown to counsel and I'm producing an envelope that has the initials,
AKJ, upon it and some writing on the
back with various dates and descrip-
tions of contents.*

banged his head on the underbody

*From that I am producing a book,
"Diving for the Body," and inside there
is apparently an inscription. Is that in
your handwriting on the inside cover?*

A   *Yes, it is.*

Q   *And that is addressed, "For Pat," and
closes, "Love, Gene, 1975," is that
correct?*

A   *Yes, that is correct.*

happy all but folded in two like a jackknife

> Q And also from that same volume I am
> producing what bears the initials AKJ
> in the top right-hand corner, an un-
> dated note. Is that in your writing?
>
> A Yes, it is.
>
> Q And that states, "Beloved, at last, a
> small gift. Love, Gene." Is that correct?
>
> A Right
>
> Q And is this what you sent to Pat
> Lowther?
>
> A Yes, it is.

never a love note

> Q I'm referring you now to what is appar-
> ently an original or top copy of a
> typewritten poem with the initials, AKJ,
> and what appears to be a carbon copy
> underneath. Now, the heading is "THE
> SUN IN NOVEMBER" and it reads, "A
> collection on green sheets kept in the
> black briefcase, found around Oct. 29,
> copy of original sent end Nov. 72." Do
> you recognize that first paragraph, Sir?
>
> A Yes, this is a poem that Pat wrote.

like the polished stainless steel of that Danish cutlery
not the traditional silver my mother has who thinks I
could do better

Q *All right, and then there is an asterisk,*
  the fourth paragraph down, and there's
  a reference there in that paragraph to,
  "In bed with you and Charles
  Bukowski, the question is: will
  Bukowski make you laugh or am i
  going to make you cry a little more
  love – close the book." Do you know
  who composed that?

a bright new sparkplug inserted

A *That also was a poem by Pat.*

Q *All right, and do you understand the*
  reference to Charles Bukowski?

A *Yes, I do, Charles Bukowski is a poet*
  from California, and Pat and I were
  reading some of his poems in a maga-
  zine. I think the name of the magazine
  is Event. She had some poems in it as
  well.

poets must share Doug's delight in making something
run with power even if it's just lines of words

Q *The bottom paragraph, Sir, refers to,*
  " . . . My lover is a Catholic with chil-
  dren in parochial schools no one i've
  loved has been ultimately any better
  for it . . . ," and is that part of a poem
  that Pat wrote, to your knowledge?

A *Yes, it is. It's part of the poem called*
  "The Sun in November."

mother says I should be unhappy waiting around but
tomorrow night music

> Q   Also an envelope date stamped Novem-
> ber 5th, 1973 addressed to Pat Lowther
> and a return address of Dorothy
> Livesay, L-I-V-E-S-A-Y, of Victoria.
> There is apparently a sketch speaking
> of Cadburo Bay and an address of
> Queenswood Drive. Are you familiar
> with that location or any of the loca-
> tions shown on that, Sir?
>
> A   I believe that is Dorothy Livesay's
> cottage.

Doug's the only guy I know who dances fast or slow
which rhymes like a poet

> Q   And did you stay on one occasion in
> Dorothy Livesay's cottage with Pat
> Lowther?
>
> A   Yes, I did, in 1973.

love the way the muscles move in his arm like solid
water and when he finally talks

> Q   And did you receive, to your knowl-
> edge, instructions from Dorothy
> Livesay as to how to get there?
>
> A   No.

"could you put it in neutral Lil and press the accelerator?"

> Q   Or did Pat?

A   No, as a matter of fact, Dorothy
     Livesay drove us there.

most guys won't let their girlfriends even sit in the
driver's seat a comfy bucket in real leather and the
handbrake not on as I take hold of the rounded

MR. DEBOU: Double A-8, Your Honour?

THE COURT: Yes.

(Letter and envelope from Dorothy Livesay
marked Exhibit A-8)

THE COURT: I take it you'll be somewhat
              longer with this witness. It's now one
              o'clock.

MR. DEBOU: Yes, Your Honour.

THE COURT: We're going to break for
              lunch time. We'll reconvene at two
              thirty. I'm going to instruct you not to
              talk to anybody with respect to this
              case and you'll be back and continue
              your direct and cross examination at
              two thirty, understood?

THE WITNESS: Yes.

THE COURT: All right, thank you.

(Witness stood down)

(PROCEEDINGS HEREUPON AD-
JOURNED TO 2:30 P.M.)

Guess I'm alone for lunch today. Elizabeth said she had a doctor's appointment. Doug's garage too far away without a car, so I'll be eating by myself for a change. Not the least bit hungry. Sometimes when he's lying next to me, I still feel alone. His hair gone funny from the way he burrows into the pillow, like he's trying to rub an itchy thought out of his head.

I haven't fixed that typo yet: *And he sad* for *said*. If you miss just one letter, you say something else. Or not even leave out a letter, but switch two of them when you type. You can write the exact opposite of what you intended: *untie* instead of *unite*. Things can go wrong too easily.

I'm the opposite of her lover. Unmarried. Shouldn't begrudge Doug his weekly visit to his ex. If he didn't see her in the hospital, would I like him less? Yet she's always there, weighing me down like an iron hat on my head.

Maybe I'll eat some Smarties. Feel like something sweet.

"Rev it some more, Lil." Afterwards, even my ears can hear the difference. The whole set of eight sparkplugs race with gleaming newness. I imagine eight sharp sparks, one right after another, flaring into the gasoline that Doug says gets squeezed into the cylinder heads before exploding the pistons backwards. Thrusts his Corvette forward, burning rubber and winding up, speeds across the Second Narrows bridge, climbs into the North Van mountains, flies up into the pure sky.

Felt high on my birthday when he surprised me, really surprised me, with this Mexican bracelet. Turquoise shells inlaid. The wide silver curve snug against my wrist bones. And after lunch at Primo's, when I had washed all the tortilla sauce off my hands, Dougie opened the *driver's* door for me. I slid in, took the black steering wheel in both hands, and couldn't believe it when he ran around to the passenger's side. He jumped in, a bit breathless – most likely scared I was going to drive off without him! Tempted more than once.

My red fingernails curling, I put the Corvette into first gear. Felt Doug watching as my red high heels slowly let up the clutch. Gently pushed down the accelerator. The sleek body gliding us through the dark streets. Didn't get nervous until it started to rain, hard. Me, a prairie girl who on occasion feels lost and gloomy under these Vancouver clouds. Like a punishment that hangs over my head for a crime I didn't do, and can't serve enough time for. Like typing a sentence that won't ever end.

But on my birthday Dougie trusted me enough to drive us all the way home, even in the downpour. He never said a word, but his eyes kept flitting between my hands and the slick road in front of the wipers thunking back and forth. Never spoke once. But every second he'd take what he thought were un-obvious glances at my hands on the steering wheel. Like it was some huge round magnet pulling his eyeballs back, again and again.

It was the same thing when we first met at my apartment. My silly roommate, Sally, had tossed my sweater into the dryer in order to free up the washer for her white load of nursey clothes. I had to tug and stretch the red wool over my head, she had shrunk it so much. And Douglas's eyes kept being tugged back to me.

Very carefully, I watched where we were going, looking ahead, braking before I had to at the intersections with red lights. The lines left by tires on the black wet road looked like lane lines. Not once did Dougie say I was a menace like some female drivers who go too slow and cause accidents.

Suddenly, a brown panel wagon with no windows in back jerked out from its parking place: right there in front of the Corvette's windshield and a car tight beside me. Thank God Doug's such a fanatic about checking his brakes. Even in the skiddy rain his car braked true. Holding its line, pulling in neither direction – and Dougie didn't lunge for the steering wheel like some dumb hero. He trusted me to get us to a safe place, so we wouldn't end up like his ex. In a hospital, unconscious for more than two years, probably forever. Drove slowly in the right-hand turning lane, until we reached home. After I turning off the ignition I began to shake like castanets.

Like this little box in my hand. I open one end, and find two yellows, an orange, and a red sitting on the cardboard lid, trapped by the angle of the fold. What are the chances of figuring out a future?

I pour them all out on the table. Who cares what people think?

Let's say the round brown ones that steal most of the light in this cafeteria are worth one, and yes. I quickly bite into the first one, taste the hard shell, and swallow it down. Then the other six dark earth pieces, counting fast, the dark candies disappearing: no yes no yes no yes.

Now the next yuckiest-looking Smarties. Banana yellow. I make them into a tree shape. Nine of them, and they will be worth two each. No-yes no-yes no-yes no-yes no-yes no-yes no-yes no-yes no-yes. Why do all the colours taste the same? Dyes.

Now for this field of Crayola grass green. These little circles of lawn will count as three apiece. No-yes-no yes-no-yes no-yes-no yes-no-yes no-yes-no yes-no-yes no-yes-no yes-no-yes no-yes-no yes-no-yes no-yes-no yes-no-yes no-yes-no.

Every Sunday afternoon he disappears for a couple of hours to view her, exactly when I'm totally free and want his company most. Guilty feelings. Usually I'm stuck here, typing someone else's words for a living. But better than her, in a coma. I don't want to think about that. Get this tightness in my throat I can't cough away sometimes, even if he's lying right beside me, his hair funny.

Only four colours left. I'll do the shiny little pumpkins next. Trick or treat? Scary masks and a haunted house. Like Carrie, she reaches a hand out from the grave at us. The orange Smarties will be worth four. Each yes-no-yes-no will end badly for me, like for the lovers in this trial. I crunch down on the sickly sweet taste. Keeping track of these words is too easy, and no fun: yes-no-yes-no yes-no-yes-no yes-no-yes-no yes-no-yes-no yes-no-yes-no yes-no-yes-no yes-no-yes-no yes-no-yes-no and the negative ending can't be avoided.

Maybe the neon pinks will cheer me up. Five. So they will go yes-no-yes-no-yes no-yes-no-yes-no yes-no-yes-no-yes nay-yea-nay-yea-nay yea-nay-yea-nay-hooray! Promising me my wishes.

Now my favourite ones, the soft Easter purples of spring that invite the eyes. They are worth six each, an even number. I can swallow them down without remembering the number of no-yes-no-yes-no-yes's because I'm still guaranteed a "yes" at the end. Doug believes it wasn't an accident. The timing was too close, he thinks, with her crashing only a day after their divorce decree.

As usual, it all depends on what's left on the table: the round valentines. It would be cheating to count them before tossing them into my mouth. They're worth seven, which means they'll keep flipping back and forth, between hope and despair, thunking like his windshield wipers. No-yes-no-yes-no-yes-no yes-no-yes-no-yes-no-yes, and I keep eating unhappy-happy-unhappy-happy-unhappy-happy-unhappy. Throwing love in between my teeth: yes-no-yes-no-yes-no-yes. But now it's a foolish, childish, ridiculous game because I can see without trying that there are only three of them left on the sweating tabletop. I'm left with a triangle, next to the empty box. A total waste of time. I put back the last three shiny red shapes that mean absolutely nothing, and shake them like a Dumbie, before dropping the box of too bright colours back into my purse.

I stand up. 2:26. Back to the courtroom, where I am a bit part in the drama. In high school I wanted to try out for the play, but was too scared I'd forget my lines or hear my voice go squeaky with everyone watching me up on the stage. A trial. Waiting to type out their lives. Like his ex-wife, duly sworn. Tomorrow night at the Body Shop Disco there will be that loud endless beat letting your brain forget. Waiting here. Late. In a coma of boredom.

2:30 p.m.

MR. DEBOU: *Recall the Lowther matter, Your Honour. Sorry for the delay. Something came up at the last moment that I wished to speak to counsel about to expedite.*

THE COURT: *I'll just remind you that you are still under oath, Sir.*

a love that didn't work out

Q   *Is this a letter that you wrote to Pat Lowther?*

A   *Yes, it is, a copy of it.*

Q   *And it reads, "Beloved, I have your letter in my hand. I put it down and begin to type. It is a poor substitute for holding you. But it's all I've got for now.*

almost like Romeo and Juliet lovers who couldn't live happily ever after

Brain Damage. Who wouldn't be in love with you? Did you say 'Macchu Picchu'" – I don't know – in –

A *"Macchu Picchu," yes.*

Q *Yes, quotation marks?*

A *That's a poem by Neruda.*

Q *All right, "Did you say 'Macchu Picchu' out loud in his presence?" And that's spelled, for the record, M-A-C-C-H-U P-I-C-C-H-U, is that correct?*

A *Yes.*

Q *And Neruda is N-E-R-U-D-A?*

A *Yes.*

MR. DEBOU: Exhibit -11?

THE COURT: Yes.

Q *In any of these letters or telephone conversations you had with Pat Lowther, did you discuss her husband?*

A *Do you mean the – well, no. I received one letter from her in which she did say something about her husband.*

could it be out of love Doug never mentions his ex?

Q *All right, we don't want to have to refer to what she said in the letter, but it concerned her husband, is that correct?*

A   Yes.

Q   And when was that?

A   I don't remember. I did give that letter
     to the Vancouver Police. I gave it to
     Detective Jorgensen.

Q   All right. And you are married?

A   That's correct, yes.

Q   And you have five children?

A   Yes.

the good and bad fortune candies

Q   And you and your family are Catholic?

A   That's correct, yes.

once I wanted to be a nun

THE COURT: Roman Catholic?

A   Roman Catholic.

Q   Did you ever discuss with Pat Lowther
     either of you leaving your families?

A   No, we didn't.

no we didn't

Q   You can now tell us what she did say on
     that September 19th conversation.

A   What I said or what –

THE COURT: What you both said.

171

Q   *What you both said.*

A   *All right. I told her about the mysterious phone call that I had received and I
wondered if there was someone in the
League of Canadian Poets that I had in
some way damaged that would be try
to be getting back at me.*

THE COURT: *Excuse me, I want you to
speak a little more slowly or pause. And
if you look at me and see me writing
away furiously, you'll pause, and then
I'll look up and you can continue
because I want to take down what you
are saying.*

A   *All right, okay.*

Q   *Now, you talked to Pat Lowther and
you spoke about this mysterious telephone call you got?*

A   *Yes.*

Q   *That you previously alluded to in your
evidence, –*

A   *Right.*

Q   *– this threatening one?*

A   *Right.*

Q   *And you wondered if someone in the
League, that is the League of Canadian*

172

Poets, yes?

A   *I wondered if someone in the League –
I was on the membership committee
and at that time we had a frozen membership and the thought went through
my head after the phone call that
perhaps someone who had been either
turned down or was still pending as a
member was angry and had chosen me
as a victim and perhaps knew about my
relationship with Pat and was using it.
So this is what I asked her on the
phone, if there was such a person, and
she said that she – she feared that it
was her husband, she feared that her
husband had been getting into her
correspondence and that he knew about
us.*

about us

Q   *Just pause there. Yes?*

A   *And until that moment this possibility
had never occurred to me. I did not
think at that time that I received the
phone call that it might be he and so it
came as a complete shock to me. And
then she said that the main – her main
concern at that time was to reassure
her husband that she was not going to
leave him and she said something to
this effect, "I can't leave him. The
children love him so." And then she*

wanted to know what I was going to do.

Q   *Just pause there, please. "I can't leave him."*

A   *The children love him so."*

no kids yet

> *Then she asked me if I were going to come to the meeting or not and I said I didn't know, I still hadn't made up my mind. Then that's the way we left it, that I still had not decided whether I was going to come or not.*

waiting for him to decide

Q   *Were you aware that at the time of September 19th, 1975 Pat Lowther was to have a manuscript that she had written, published?*

A   *She told me that Oxford University press had made a tentative offer on her next manuscript, "A Stone Diary," yes.*

yes wanting him to make up his mind yes

Q   *In your mind, as a result of this telephone conversation on September 19th, 1975, did it appear to you that this conference was something that was important to Pat Lowther?*

important soon to make up my own

A   *Yes, it was very important to her.*

Q   *In your mind would Pat Lowther have*

*left her two children if she was leaving
her husband Roy Lowther or taken
them with her, can you say?*

A   *Pardon? I didn't understand your
question –*

Q   *All right. On the basis of these conversations and correspondence that you
had had with Pat Lowther up to and
including the September 19th telephone
conversation, in your mind did it appear to you that Pat Lowther would, if
she left her husband, take her children
or leave her children there?*

A   *I think she would have taken her
children, yes.*

Q   *And after this telephone conversation
of September 19th, 1975, did you ever
see or speak to Pat Lowther again?*

A   *No, I didn't.*

she might have gone dancing tomorrow night

MR. DEBOU: *Your witness.*

175

Reflecting Sunglasses

Circles of sky
and storefronts in my face –
look through me:
lattice of moving air
chrome sunburst faces –
I'm a see-through woman
proof enough of
the proposition that we're all
mostly
empty space.
I swing along carrying
tunnels of vision
through the imaginary fabric
of my brain.
Lean closer and you'll see
you looking out
from me.

• Pat Lowther

from "Notes on 'Notes From Furry Creek'"

Canadian Literature #155, Winter 1997
Keith Harrison

Notes From Furry Creek

I

The water reflecting cedars
all the way up
deep sonorous green –
nothing prepares you
for the ruler-straight
log fallen across
and the perfect
water fall it makes
and the pool behind it
Novocain-cold
and the huckleberries
hanging
like fat red lanterns

II

The dam, built
by coolies, has outlived
its time; its wall
stained sallow
as ancient skin
dries in the sun

The spillway still
splashes bright spray
on the lion
shapes of rock
far down below

The dam foot
is a pit
for the royal animals
quiet and dangerous
in the stare
of sun and water

III

When the stones swallowed me
I could not surface
but squatted
in foaming water
all one curve
motionless,
glowing like agate.

I understood the secret
of a monkey-puzzle tree
by knowing its opposite:

the smooth and the smooth
and the smooth takes,
seduces your eyes
to smaller and smaller
ellipses;
reaching the centre

you become
stone, the perpetual
lavèd god.

Title:

- notes are parts of songs too. cf. her music poem, "In The Silence Between": "It is as if huge / migrations take place / between the steps / of music / like round / stones in water: / what flows between is / motion so constant / it seems still"

- notes fragments of whole but plural, multiple (vague index to three parts of poem's structure), bits of knowledge, role of observer as learner – perception preceding/proceeding without hypothesis

- Since Keats's odes, title prepositions crucial to tell how emotions fit with objects in space: "to a nightingale," romantic address, cry for communion, lyric apostrophe of transcendence and ironic gap vs. "on a Grecian Urn," reflection upon, meditation about. For Lowther, "From." What can be taken away, as well as derived, and also maybe (a sense of failure?) at a distance, an artistic remove from source

- a name, creek – north of Vancouver, with "Furry," soft and warm, colliding with expectations of mountain coldness. Animal presence implied, threat of bears, fury? Or something undrinkable. [But my neighbour on Hornby Island, Marilyn Mullan, who's just retired as head of the mining museum at Britannia Beach (a couple of miles further north) says Oliver Furry was a trapper, grub-staked by furriers in Vancouver hoping to find gold; he followed Dr. Forbes (a medical doctor who did prospecting on the side) and staked claims and worked for gold at Britannia in 1890's, until a syndicate was formed out of early claim-holders to raise capital to mine. (Involved Moodie, railway figure and son of literary Susanna. His daughter interviewed as an old woman > never allowed to play with other kids: snobbery across the generations.) New York interests bought out first syndicate at Britannia Beach, and developed a mine that produced a little gold, and a huge amount of copper.]

Section I

- "The water reflecting cedars" – precise present participle observation, mirror theme (see her "I.D." & "Reflecting sunglasses") merging of land and water (with air in reach of trees into sky) an echoing fullness, unity of nature & world – cedar the emblem of West Coast; native arts of making: canoe, poles, lodge, basketry

- "all the way up" – perfectly, heaven implicit [conventions of no caps at start of lines (ex-

cept for beginning of sentence that becomes
note #1) and no line-stop punct. until last sec-
tion]

- "deep sonorous green – " back to musicality,
  double harmony metaphor through inter-
  fusion of sight and sound, the synaesthesia of
  "deep" as both bass note and intensifier of colour of life; experience of senses felt and anato-
  mized at once, "reflected" upon, while the dash
  typographically updates the "O" of Romantic
  identification, or alerts us to a haiku-like shift

- "nothing prepares you" > anxiety, fear of future, a foreboding, acknowl. of inability to cope,
  startled as the line floats off into blankness, or
  future words. [With this phrase, hard not to
  remember that her husband threw her murdered body into Furry Creek: "What came to
  me was Furry Creek. Now I've loved it all my
  life. I know it like the back of my hand. My
  father worked there 25 years. I was raised in
  Britannia Beach a short distance away, and my
  wife and I spent some of our honeymoon
  there . . . " Roy Lowther, *Appeal Book* 353]

- "the ruler-straight" order of geometric line and
  human measurement vs. the drooping, taper-
  ing sprays of fan-like cedar branches. Comments on the opening image/sound; "log fallen
  across" > noun comes after the line break, the
  thing that falls into reader's line of sight after
  delay, but this line ends with a prep. leading to

expectation of more: "across" what? Never given because another perception is recorded instead in rush and discontinuity of note-taking

- Though "fallen" and "log" signify mortality, an image of a bridge here & the next line, "and the perfect," counterpoints with sense of awe, so neg. and pos. alternate, form emotional rhythm that gives context to "water fall it makes," where separation of morphemes restores the separateness of thing and act, so "makes" becomes a creative shaping, the Maker, the immanent God of "Tintern Abbey" (Wye=Furry), as inspiration for the poet as "maker" (cf. her "Inheritance": "a long life of making")

- "and the pool behind it" through parallelism implied as perfect too; "pool" felt as a <u>verbal</u>, an action as much as a thing, because of prior separation of "water fall"?

- "Novocain-cold" sense of touch, unfeeling feel, implies swimming/bathing/immersion, and dental assoc. paradox: painful needle to kill pain

- "and the huckleberries" taste sensation, assoc. with escape from civiliz. fraud, "Lighting out for the territories" of Huck converges with escapism of Romantics, breathless quality of repeated coordinate conjunction > a naïve syntax of child-like innocence, a pure responsiveness to sensations, ordering newness

- "hanging" ominous, anticipative, like reader before concluding line, suspended between sky and water – observer, as in opening lines; "like fat red lanterns" illumination, "fat" a neg. word given sense of abundance; delicious, ample light, enough to navigate by, festive welcome

- no period at end because no terminating stoppage; process of green nature sonorous, sounding on. [cf. Pat Lowther's mother's remark: "'She seemed to grow by herself. She was no trouble. She just grew'" (back cover of *Final Instructions*). In last word, upbeat ending of brightness linked to human design, "lantern" as human object, along with "ruler" and "Novocain," offer tropes of measure, curing of pain, restorative light: edenic

Section II

- "The dam, built" – opp. the one made by fallen log, the pause of comma to split product and process; obstruction of Nature's flow def. of human creation? ["I was headed for South Valley dam. There was a dam on Furry Creek. It's called Furry Creek dam. We call it South Valley Dam. My father looked after it for 25 years." Roy Lowther 359]

- "by coolies, has outlived" the shock of lang., the casual racism, oppression, esp. in natural setting, post-edenic consciousness now, made <u>concrete</u> in origins of dam, the colonial history of West Coast North America, the exploitation of Chinese, but inanimate has "outlived" the builders, a kind of monument to human effort; the what delayed: "its time; its wall" its limits of usefulness, wall of prejudice & also metaphor of time as confinement & evoking China civilizing achiev. of Great Wall against "stained sallow" – almost pathetic fallacy where object takes on "colouration," pale yellow of workers, and moral "stain" of "whites" > the BC female writer's fascination with cultural otherness of Chinese: Pat Lowther's poem, "The Chinese Greengrocers" [now in *Time Capsule*], bits of Emily Carr's autobiography, Ethel Wilson's *Swamp Angel*, Marilyn Bowering's novel, *To All Appearances a Lady*: a long essay to be written about representing gender through ethnicity?

- "as ancient skin" – personified as if the thing had become its builders; as if technology had been returned to origin in human bodies; "dries in the sun" to become opp. of creek

- Stanza break, new sent. & "The spillway still" ambig. and oxymoron: structure there, but no water flows over it > life <u>and</u> immobility, but next line "splashes bright spray": action light wetness, "on the lion": animate form of predator menaces in "shapes of rock" and we're back

184

to the unmoving, now "far down below" the creek's reflecting surface. [Now relative wilderness has become a golf course & condominium development: "The hardest part of playing Furry creek is keeping your eye on the ball. Superior golf requires intense concentration, particularly when playing the most beautiful course from sea to sky on earth. But bearing this in mind, we've designed our 6,200 yard all-terrain masterpiece to be as forgiving as it is challenging" (brochure bumf) > but I found in Furry Creek a hard, dimpled ball, with black letters, "LEGEND"]

- stanza three – "The dam foot" (like a comic curse) "is a pit," a metaphor of death, Dante's hell or Poe's confinement > paradisal feel of first section undercut; "for the royal animals" brings back lions, and (zoomorphic?) impulse of humans to create recognizable shapes; cognitively and aesthetically imprison; "quiet and dangerous" noise from spillway water, not from (un)roaring animals, making menace more menacing > because "nothing prepares you"

- setting is dramatized in conflictual terms – switch from "coolies," racism, etc. to animals that can hurt "in the stare," scopic; merely cinematic fear, a playful illusion in reflecting watcher? The "sun and water" in a stand-off, with the bystanding "I" not openly part of poem yet

Section III

- "When the stones swallowed me" – threat of lions seemingly fulfilled here, 1st person pronoun > initial use as <u>object</u> of action, in past tense, so dramatic episode itself omitted; a Jonah hint of miraculous survival?

- "I could not surface" evokes Atwood, with some of the same R. D. Laing sense of drowning in depths as preferable to being superficial, but the personal can't fuse with Nature, except temporarily: "squatted" > not erect like trees; also a trespass, to stay on property of another, i.e., remain outside a legal or natural belonging

- "in foaming water" angry, again precisely observed detail of fall, foaming at mouth=madness? > sounds before and after the making of words; "all one curve" curl of body, curve of spray of water, human and water together in a visual echo, (sub)merging

- "motionless," body like rocks, unlike water, 1st comma at end of line to emphasize that stillness, but "glowing like agate" > from death to light, psych. reversal & an echo of lanterns

- first period in poem, rock-certainty, shining exhilaration, *satori*

- st.2 – "I understood the secret" universal, mystical, unqualified (until next line); "of a monkey-puzzle tree" – a little bathos, puzzlement; the one tree that supposedly monkeys can't climb because of spikey texture, maximum surface [Iain Higgins, editor of this essay at <u>Can</u>. <u>Lit</u>., writes in the margins here, "note too the "<u>a</u>" (not <u>the</u>)" [insight coming from and to the particular, not via Platonic Ideal?] & "also totally out of context, no? this is cedar/fir country" [bleak paradox: urban consciousness displaces, alienates, even as it connects?]]

- "by knowing its opposite:" – her colon promising an answer, the riddle about to be resolved > progression in poem from observation to imaginative engagement to immersion to illumination

- st.3 – "the smooth and the smooth" rep. as emph., and washings of wonderment; "and the smooth takes," loss, erodes, eliminates the superfluous, discovers essential form within; "seduces your eyes" > 2nd pers. pl. evasion & appeal to common experience when it's particular; "I" again, but enlarged, shared: "Like Neruda, Lowther knows that it 'isn't easy / to keep moving thru / the perpetual motion / of surfaces' in a world w[h]ere the bodies are 'laid / stone upon stone'; but the process is necessary: 'You are changing, Pablo, becoming an element / a close throat of quartz / a calyx / imperishable in earth.' At the psychological level, Lowther's preoccupation with stone, the most resistant of the things in the physical world, represents a desire to eliminate the surfaces, edges, boundaries that separate [hu]man from [hu]man and [hu]man from objects in nature" (Geddes *15 Canadian Poets plus 5* 395)

- "to smaller and smaller" stones?, more acute, minute and exact perception > "ellipses," of course the eyes' own shape, so organs of perceiver and perceived, self and world, "<u>reflect</u>" each other, as in opening lines of cedar and water

- "reaching the centre" – not *at* the centre, but getting towards it like Tantalus grasping; away from periphery, nearer core: in-site/insight

- "you become" – what? By truncating the line, a teleological statement offered, but aim left off, as if process itself is purpose > the condition of being alive which includes old self being swallowed, over and over

- But with "stone, the perpetual," the shock of death-like fixity > hard, inanimate, unfeeling yet immortal. A horror image, but monumental, like "coolies'" dam (bad pun on Grand Coulee dam?); "stoned": 60s vocab. here in altered state of consciousness, beyond prosaic reality that stones usually represent (cf.

Samuel Johnson's kicking a stone: "Thus I refute Bishop Berkeley"); Pat Lowther's '74 collection called *Milk Stone*, in the midst of such contemporary Western Canadian poetry publishers as The Very Stone Press (?) & Turnstone Press, and – long before Carol Shield's novel, *The Stone Diaries* – "Notes From Furry Creek" was posthumously printed in *A Stone Diary*

- "lavèd god." 2nd period, archaic word, musical emphasis, Romantic diction, Keats? > Pat Lowther's neg. capability to look outside the window and be – not sparrow pecking around in gravel – animate & too easy! – but the <u>gravel</u> itself, the small rocks. A passive giving of self to l.c. pantheistic god in washing by Furry Creek; eternal in process of cleansing, renewal [S.O.E.D. "Now chiefly *poet.*1. *trans.* To wash, bathe. . . . 2. *trans.* Of a body of water; To wash against, to flow along or past"]

- An ending in which I can "explain" every word, but somehow I'm left outside; not washed clean by cosmic consciousness: Why this balking? Is it something in the poem, or a flawed reading, or does this sense of emotional strandedness reveal the limits of communicability, or just follow from the particular slant of my life (where Death, a heavy stone flung at the forehead, knocks out certain kinds of signif. and enchantment along with the living daylights), or is the balked response at the poem's close

due to an obtruding biographical awareness >
["Cases of domestic violence against women
resulting in murder are so commonplace they
have taken on a horrific banality ... leaving
them [the children] alone to piece together a
history from amongst the wreckage." Beth
Lowther, in letter requesting access to sealed
documents marked "Exhibits"]

February 21st, 1997

Dear Keith:

My apologies for not contacting you sooner; the joint's been really jumping lately. Firstly, I want to thank you for sending me a copy of 'Notes on Notes.' It has made the rounds in our family and we are all very pleased with it. I've taken the liberty of enclosing a copy of my proposed introduction for Time Capsule. Actually, it has since been accepted, but since it hasn't been revised, you'll forgive me if it's cliché-ridden!

My antennae went up a number of times while reading your paper. I believe you're talking about getting to the physical response to the mind's act of recognition. This was what my mother always strove for. When I use the term 'bodily intelligence,' I mean that the experience of the mind is writ small on the body. There is a link between the two that goes beyond the nervous system. Mum knew this. Survivors of trauma recognize the concept of body memory; no matter how we try to shelve our experiences, our bodies say 'No, look: this happened here, and here, and here.' The pleasure experienced in the body when a concept becomes illuminated in the mind could be described as the work of some primeval sub-epidermal brain (like a Gaia theory of the body!). I think my mother knew this instinctively. The point is, all divisions are imposed; arbitrary. The links are what count.

So, it seems apparent you are a kindred spirit, and in view of that I hope you'll be able to attend the book launch set to happen at Havana Restaurant on Commercial Drive on May 31st. We'll send you an invitation as soon as they're printed.

Thank you again for sending us your paper (you can see it has had the desired effect on one reader at least) and do call us when you're in town, or if you need another look at mum's notes, etc. Hope classes are going well.

Yours in Subversive Thought,
Beth & Co.

(Proposed Introduction to Time Capsule)

If I should live to be 100, I will spend much of each
day thinking of my mother Pat, a woman I knew for
only nine years. I have come to believe she understood
the particular resonance of synchronous events in time;
its non-linearity, its similarity to an organic form such
as an arbutus tree (her favourite), sending branches
forward and unfurling its leaves, its smooth red bark
peeling back layer after layer with the seasons.

That is why three years ago, when a chance excur-
sion into my brother Alan's attic yielded parts of a
manuscript she had written called **Time Capsule**, I was
astounded at what the discovery signified, but I was
not surprised. Not that my mother had premonitory
knowledge of the future or an extrasensory knowledge of time, but that she brought her considerable
intellect to bear on the subject, and reached an
attunement with time that many of us are perhaps
lacking. She thought, with joy and gusto, and sent her
thoughts gallivanting across the universe.

Pat Lowther never believed in a dichotomous split
of mind over body. She saw the physical union of human beings as a holy sacrament, and she had a deep
reverence for what might be termed the 'bodily intelligence' of non-human life forms; the ability of the
octopus to learn by observation, for example. (She once
said: "I'm having a tremendous love affair with inver-
tebrates!")

Historically, the equation of women with carnal knowledge has caused us untold suffering. Similarly, the man who would take her life was deeply threatened by her frank openness to sexuality. Perhaps, inasmuch as all women living with a violent spouse carry, like a virus, the possibility of their own deaths inside them, she knew, and subconsciously began making preparations. And so, the manuscript was written and sent into time, like a stone dropped into water, sending ripples which would wash over us twenty years later, spreading outward with the message: I am still with you.

If we, the children of Pat Lowther, should accomplish little else with our time here on earth, I know this act alone will bring us peace: we send these poems out to the four corners, her words which he tried to take away from us, her voice which would not be silenced. We send these words back out to the world, and to you.

> 'Now that your ashes have been given
> to the wind,
> times when I breathe
> a sudden atom of sourceless laughter
> I shall acknowledge you,
> my friend.'
> Beth Lowther
> January 1997

from **Division**

When our mouths have slid apart
from the last blurred kiss
and landed, quenched, in pillows,
he closes on a private agony
and sends his last thick, thumbing thought from me.
O even lulled in billows
of warm-wave loving, I know this:
Flesh has not healed his scissored heart.

• Pat Lowther

Tuesday, April 19, 1977

Everyone in the courtroom – the judge, despite having a spot of trouble with his voice, the prosecutor who uses folksy language to try to get us on his side, the typist with her perfectly straight back in a white blouse that's too tight, even me, Susan Morgan, juror number seven – has a sense of what we're doing here, but after nearly a week Roy Lowther still looks awkward. He's finally getting his say, standing up on the courtroom floor in his blue suit, but it's like he can't decide whether to get mad or cry.

> *Then I resolved to go to the poetry reading, to stand up from the floor and demand twenty minutes to read, and two, to have some socialist friends there to back me up, and three, to take the poems I had already chosen to read, put them on a broad sheet on our Gestetner machine and give them out at the door. I stayed at Little Mountain about two hours. I saw no one that I knew there.*

*This was Wednesday morning. I talked
to no one. It was a fine day, there was
quite a bit of cloud.*

Which was it: cloudy or sunny?

Mr. Henderson, the handsome defence lawyer nick-
named "Ace," has the same air of confidence as my
ex-husband – his poker-face doesn't show that his cli-
ent might have flubbed.

*About 11:30 I got back home. I made no
stops on the way. I heard no sound at
all, checked the main floor. No one was
there, so I went upstairs and I glanced
into the work room, went into our
room, looking to see if she was up and
how she was feeling. In the bedroom,
standing by the grey box I saw there
she was, nothing on except a blouse
with a pink flowered pattern, something she had bought in July. The
blankets were pulled back neatly. The
bottom was pulled back, the body was
lying with no blanket on it, pale yellow
pallor of her body, no marks on the
body or the face or one side of the head.
Other side head covered with blood.
Two-thirds of the ceiling, the red wall,
blood everywhere. I concluded someone
had come in, hit her on the head, I
don't know what with.*

There's been endless discussion of the hammer. A
dozen voices that have already testified flash through
my mind – like I'm still at work supervising the switch-

board. Next to me, Mr. Dadrian, juror number eight, shifts his long, grey-flannelled legs.

> *I sat down on the grey box and I stared and was stunned. I don't know how long I sat there, not very long. Pity came like a wave. She was dead, the woman who was one of the finest poets in this country that it will ever have, one of the best organizers, she had a tremendous love affair going. It was the real thing. She had been my wife for twelve years. I loved her to the end, not as much as at the beginning of the marriage.*

I don't doubt he loved his wife once. On the back of that photo we saw entered into evidence, Roy Lowther wrote, "Glamour puss at Phantom Lake. Summer of 1964." In a month of Sundays Barry wouldn't have called me a glamour puss. Though he did call me "Honey" when we were still trying to have a family. And maybe a few more times after he gave up.

> *Second wave came over me, I had walked into this trap of all time. It was known that ours was not a good marriage. I knew that the husband would be the first suspect.*

I never suspected. Blind-sided. It was too soon. Just after our sailing adventure in a rented Cal 25 where we managed to fix the bilge pump together, mapped out an unfamiliar coastline, and drank a bottle of Mumm's champagne when we got to our destination:

Desolation Sound. Barry amazed and delighted at how skilled I was at watercolours. We had sailed right past Furry Creek.

> *I felt that if I went to the police that I would be arrested on the spot and I believe that to this day.*

Credible motive for the attempted cover-up? Or just some concocted story? Barry's lawyer turned black into white while I sat there, my hair going grey.

> *Then I was aware of the feeling of resentment towards society. Somebody she let in or somebody had broken in through the front door. I had no idea of the weapon, I never thought of a hammer. I felt that I had two options: one, the police, or two, confiscate the body.*

"Confiscate" isn't the right word. Why's he trying to sound like some kind of official?

> *I did not plan it out. I just did one thing and the next and the next.*

Like the love and the marriage and the divorce. Why hide his wife's body if he's innocent?

> *I thought it would have to be in a place that I knew and to which I had access and unfrequented.*

I feel a migraine lurking behind my eyes. Underwater blur coming on. For five years now I've tried to swim away from him. But strands of thought drag, my head trails yellow-green memories like seaweed.

> *I knew the area like the back of my*

hand, I decided on Furry Creek.

One of the photos, looking upstream from the highway bridge, showed Furry Creek and their campsite, in about 1965, near their beginning. Near the mouth. Relationships now, like campsites, only of temporary use?

> *I wanted to get rid of the blood; it was all over everything.*

He loved her, lost her, killed her. Keep an open mind, Susie. As juror number seven, you've sworn to hear all the evidence first. He said he panicked at the sight of her bloody body that he thought would unfairly incriminate him. You've made decisions on the spur of the moment too.

> *All in the full moon. The car was in a little strip of land between the garage and the lane.*

On the witness stand, Roy Lowther has quite a dramatic flair. But an accused person isn't supposed to be acting?

> *The body was quite difficult to move because of rigor mortis. It was clothed and it was in a sheet, in a grey blanket.*

The detective said it was found naked.

> *I put it in the car trunk. It is now three or four in the morning. I then went upstairs into the front bedroom for the blue mattress. It was a heavy mattress, but I imagine I moved it in the same*

way, the same route, but I overbalanced
on the back stairs and the mattress and
I fell down together.

It's like horror and slapstick at the same time.

At Furry Creek, I opened the trunk,
took Pat out first.

Mr. Dadrian gasps.

The cardboard box was in the back seat.
I don't think I put the box in the trunk.
I most likely left it in the house until I
left at 9 a.m. I took the body out of the
trunk. The car was parked about two
car lengths up from the gravel road,
partly obscured by trees. I tried to carry
the body, I dragged it by the waist, but I
could not get it up to the dam. I had to
give that up.

There's uncontradicted evidence that Mrs. Lowther was having an affair. After what that two-timing Barry put me through, I should be sympathetic to the defendant. Made the wrong connection by introducing my bimbo cousin with brassy hair to my husband. Roy Lowther knew back in 1974 that another man had written a poem about kissing the stretch marks on his wife's belly, yet the murder occurred a year later. Why? I am only one of twelve, seated on the edge of the jury box.

Where the road became a path, that is
fifty, seventy-five or a hundred feet up,
the road becomes a path where some
rocks appear on it. The side of the road

drops sharply to the Creek at a bend in the Creek. I saw where I could drop her down there, so long as she remained there, she would not be seen.

For nearly a year I saw, and didn't want to see. Desolate.

It was a twenty or twenty-five foot drop, broken by tree roots. I took the blanket and the sheet off. That left a clothed body. It dropped away gently onto a flat rock beside the water. When the water rises, it flows over that rock. The water was three feet below where the body was lodged. When I left the body, I expected that she would remain there throughout the winter in the snow. I should have known. I did not expect that the body would be washed away. I did not think the Creek would rise that much.

Beside me, Mr. Dadrian breathes out loudly. His crazy eyebrows visible from the corner of my eye. Pretty soon my migraine is going to hit. My head won't be able to handle the insistent buzz of human voices much longer. Like Roy Lowther's now. He moves out of their Vancouver house, and takes their children to Mayne Island because he …

… couldn't stand it anymore without her.

A superhuman effort to keep my aching eyes open. Pat had migraines too. A splitting headache. Testimony earlier that the defendant tried to break his own head open:

> *(I've seen him bend the lids of pots. I've seen him break dishes. I've seen him smash or crack doors with his fists. And I've also seen him bang his head on the wall.)*

We'd all be better off as brainless slugs.

> *I brought the hammer over to Mayne.*

The murder weapon again – like a stuck record.

> *The detective asked if I could give an explanation and I could not, and I cannot give any now, unless it was used by the killer.*

If Roy Lowther used the hammer to kill his wife, why didn't he just heave it into the ocean? When the policeman asked to see it, the hammer was on the wall right across from where the detective was sitting! Like that story we read in school by Edgar Allan Poe – "The Purloined Letter." The clever detective deduces that the stolen letter must be concealed through some kind of obvious display.

How much longer is it before I can get back to the jury room for some medication?

It turned out to be one gigantic headache, but I gave Barry the benefit of the doubt in Montréal because our whole country had, at last, fallen head-over-heels in love with itself. During the summer of Expo '67 everyone was bubbling over with happiness.

How can cold turn into hot for millions of people all at once, and make love boil up to the surface? And where does all that love evaporate? Into the sky, which could be grey or black or even blue? For me, it was a rainy, luckless Saturday night at Horseshoe Bay, waiting hour after hour in the ferry parking lot for a man who'd decided to stay on the other side of the Gulf.

Spots form before my eyes. His lawyer very good at defending the undefendable. A future judge? The cross-examination still to come. After a break, please! The electrical storm in my head building.

Susie, you've got to force yourself to listen – and keep an open mind. You're not supposed to have already made your mind up like a neatened bed. The pillows plumped, the sheet folded back smartly. Hard not to, after the testimony by Pat's mother:

> *(He brought his hand down on the*
> *table hard and he stood up and the*
> *chair toppled backwards and he said,*
> *"No other man will get her," and he*
> *walked out of the room)*

Hear ringing in my ears now. It will be a huge relief when this trial's over to get back to work at B.C. Tel – or, better yet, call in sick. Electric words from days ago keep plugging themselves inside my brain:

> *(He had tears in his eyes several times.*
> *He sat at the kitchen table and spoke to*
> *the children and cried and then he left*
> *and walked out into the woods and the*
> *children ran after him crying. Nobody*
> *knew just why)*

Even after my lawyer told me I had to stop, I kept crying into the phone, stupidly. But finally I learned the painter's technique of not washing out what you've done with too much water. At least half the world must drown in Phantom Lake.

Testimony slops around in my head like oily bilge-water. My dizzied brain can't take any more. It's been crammed too full.

> *(I remember when their first child was about one, Roy was feeding her in her crib and she was crying and he kept feeding her and she started to choke)*

Is the Judge looking at me?

> *(She tried to take the food from Roy and he jumped up and hit her with his arm, sending her from the kitchen into the dining room and backwards over a chair)*

My hand pressed against my hot forehead doesn't help. Juror number eight glances at me, his mouth half-open.

> *I think we will adjourn until two o'clock this afternoon. I think, but I am not sure – I think we will be in room 318. You recall the warning.*

Recall words of lost happiness.

> *(She had a thing about Furry Creek. We used to go picnicking there.)*

Recall how Barry would fetch my headache pill and a not-too-cold glass of water – remember how our two lengths matched perfectly in bed. After making love, we would curl together drowsily. Lying on our sides. Even in sleep, when one of our bodies turned, the other one would roll over too. Giving and receiving comfort all through the night.

98 12 10

Dear Keith

Wishing you a happy solstice / Xmas / Yule / New Year. Beth told me about your meeting with her. Sounds <u>exciting</u>. Please keep me posted! Thanks.

Chris Lowther

PAT LOWTHER'S

TIME CAPSULE

TO BE UNVEILED

SATURDAY, MAY 31, 1997

A Daughter's Search

Introduction by Christine Lowther

Children sense adult's otherworldliness as well as their unavailability. I resented trying to catch Mother's attention when she was lost in her poetry. She was off exploring other worlds, creating new languages of expression, when I wanted praise for my drawing. Sometimes I'd wake in the night to see her uncanny head leaning around the doorway, silhouetted against the hall light. How long had she been there? She made no sound; she would perhaps be swaying ever so slightly. I dared not call out to this strange being.

After her murder I would often dream of opening a closet and finding her. She stood, again slightly swaying, with even more of a faraway look in her eyes, her mouth open. Unseeing, unhearing. In the dream it was decided (by one or another family member) that my mother was 'on her way to heaven.' For some reason, this closet was one of her stops along the way. I obediently shut the door, or woke up.

When I was in the womb, my mother read poetry at rallies against the Vietnam war. Five years later, she took us to a demonstration to save two big old trees near where we lived in south Vancouver. She was gone two years later, leaving a legacy of keys to her mystery: her poems. And she is always with me, in my activism and when I write, urging me on: an encouraging and inspiring voice.

It is difficult to not talk about violence and tragedy when mulling over the life and death of my mother. But this is a happy occasion; this is a triumphant book. Perhaps it is enough for now to remember that domestic terrorism has robbed Canada of a gifted poet, as well as robbing the poet of her life.

Several years ago I was given a tape of my mother reading her poetry. I was surprised to hear a much higher voice than I remembered (or imagined). A recording-musician friend played the tape on his equipment, and revealed that I was listening to it at the wrong speed. He corrected it, and played it again. As my mother's true voice sounded from the speakers, goose bumps prickled on the back of my neck.

I began actively searching for information after the twenty-year memorial in Toronto in June 1995, which was organized by Toby Brooks and Della Golland, who wrote her MA thesis on Pat's poetry. I now have a bulging file that requires effort to snap close. Still, there are no colour photographs, no films of my mother reading her poetry. Or are there? The discovery of late unpublished poems and the birth of this book seem to be a sign. My search will continue.

Christine Lowther
March 1997

Afterward

Writing the Unwritable

"A beginning is an artifice, and what recommends one over another is how much sense it makes of what follows."

Ian McEwan – *Enduring Love*

Did *Furry Creek*, my non-fiction novel, start in 1975, here?

BODY IDENTITY CONFIRMED

Homicide detectives have positively identified the body found last week near Squamish as missing poet Pat Lowther, 40, who disappeared from her Vancouver home. She had apparently been killed by a head blow which fractured her skull. The badly decomposed remains, pulled out of Furry Creek on Monday . . .

Or did my documentary imaginings of a poet's life and art begin on a cold, clear day in Montréal in the mid-seventies when I slid into the warmth of Classic Bookstore and came across Pat Lowther's imagistic work which took me back to my West Coast origins, causing me to talk ardently about such poems as "Coast Range" and "Notes from Furry Creek" in my classes at Dawson College, without any awareness of her murder?

Or did this non-fiction novel originate in 1996 as a small square of pale-blue sticky paper on a narrow wooden banister?

Back on the West Coast by then, I had had this shakey impulse to explore Pat Lowther's poetry and biography. I visited the Vancouver Courthouse looking for trial transcripts, and was stunned to find that such legal records were rarely made available, often no longer existed.

A helpful clerk advised me to write to the Associate Chief Justice of B.C. and request permission to view the existing, relevant documents, but warned me to expect a refusal. In a brief letter I offered my credentials (books, degrees) and explained my motives (the creation of a work fusing fiction with fact), then returned home to Hornby Island where I waited for an answer. Hearing nothing, I impatiently set out once more on the three-ferry-ride journey to Vancouver, hoping to turn up some useful material in the UBC Library, though inwardly getting ready to abandon a project which, in any case, posed artistic and ethical questions that were likely unanswerable.

Arriving in the city, dopey with fatigue, I let myself into my father-in-law's house, where I noticed the message on the banister, "Keith, phone Beth Lowther," along with a number.

My feelings were instant, varied, and intense. Desiring uncomplicated imaginative freedom from actual lives and not wishing to be too intrusive, I had had no desire to contact members of Pat Lowther's family. Why had this stranger with her resonant last name suddenly called me? I felt guilt-induced anxiety about being revealed as unworthy, even an absurd sense of let-down at being reminded by a mere name that it obviously wasn't my story, but what I felt most was elation because out of nowhere had come a wonderful connective gesture, a gift.

Yet what was I doing trying to imagine a fictive shape for Pat Lowther's actual life? How could I talk on the phone other than falsely to someone whose mother had been murdered by her father?

I called the number on the blue square of paper. Beth, the young woman who answered, was articulate and friendly and attentive, and (I sensed) was skilfully interviewing me. I mentioned *Eyemouth*, my novel, set mainly in Scotland during the French revolution and taking the form of letters. She mentioned her admiration for Rosemary Sullivan's biography of Gwendolyn MacEwen, and asked that in any writing I did on Pat Lowther that her mother be treated with honesty and respect. Beth informed me that her mother, just before the murder, had prepared for publication a group of new poems called "Time Capsule," recently discovered in her brother's attic. Seeking in the court records a possible photograph of her mother for use in a post-humous publication of this material, Beth had been in the chambers of the Associate Chief Justice the day my letter of request had arrived, and he had passed it on to her. Coincidence or synchronicity?

The first time I met Beth in Vancouver she showed me a picture of an exuberantly young great-aunt who had been a dancer in the fabled Rockettes, and another one (I think) of her maternal grandmother, and a photograph in a simple frame that I had seen on the back of books: her camera-shy mother. Beth told me she had liked my novel, *Eyemouth,* and had bought two copies, sending one to her sister, Christine, who lived in Tofino. Then Beth pulled out several large cardboard boxes. She insisted I borrow copies of her mother's unpublished poems, xeroxes of Pat Lowther's journal, bound trial transcripts, love letters. . . .

I felt she was being too generous, trusting me way too much.

Back at Hornby Island, I decided to start writing my non-fiction novel where my interest had begun, with the poetry of Pat Lowther. I wished to respect the artist before I faced the melodrama of her death (although smuggling literary criticism into my project would ensure that my book, if ever completed and published, would find fewer readers). In responding newly to the short lines of her poem, "Notes on Furry Creek," I found myself taking notes. Afterwards, I balked at smoothing my jotted flashes into a sustained essay. I wanted to keep the at-risk sense of excitement of trying to sort out what was going on as it was going on;

any polished essay would betray that feeling of being both breathless and breathing inside her river of words.

I tried field notes as a way of setting down that feeling of aliveness. The reader as critic, like an on-site geologist, who cleaves open a rock, hoping perhaps to find a fossil – a life-form that persists as a bodied image – and in a small notebook makes quick notations about location, depth, density, mineral mix, colours. Even as rain-water is washing the dirt off the writing hand to mix with the fluid ink of jottings. Before cleaning up, expanding, organizing such field notes, before hiding fragmentary thoughts in shapely sentences and editing out stray emotions via correct paragraphs, a writer might record an intimate encounter with a poem. In any event, I typed up this piece, "Notes on 'Notes on Furry Creek,'" and sent it off to Beth Lowther, and to *Canadian Literature*, which, to my delighted surprise, wanted to publish it right away (the first scholarly article on Pat Lowther's work, according to the *PMLA* bibliography, in ten years). In February of 1997 I received the letter signed "Beth & Co," reporting the "essay" had "made the rounds in the family and they were all very pleased with it." Beth enclosed her introduction to *Time Capsule*, and invited me to its launch on May 31, at the Havana Restaurant.

Not since Leonard Cohen read at UBC in the mid-sixties has there been such a turnaway crowd for poetry in Vancouver.

Afterwards, I talked to a very happy Beth. She suggested I introduce myself to her sister. I went over to

Christine, but before I could speak, she said, "Hi, Keith." I asked her how she recognized me, since my author's photo on *Eyemouth* had a beard and I was now shaven. She said, "Your eyebrows." We both laughed, and she signed her name to my copy of *Time Capsule*, crossing out the printed word, "Christine," in her "Introduction," and substituting "Chris." I went back to my island, grateful for the candid warmth of Pat Lowther's two daughters.

Hiding out from visitors at Hornby, I wrote another segment of my projected book, this time fusing criticism with fiction, focusing on the extraordinary prose poem of Pat Lowther's called "The Face." I titled this "Black Rainbows (non-non-fiction)."

At one stage I lost my desire to continue writing. Pat Lowther's death was unwritable anyway. Why hadn't I begun a novel on windsurfing? Or why didn't I just hang out at the ball park and swing a bat with the Hornby Eagles? I nearly abandoned Furry Creek.

Instead, I eased myself out from underneath some of the palpable weight of actual lives by retreating to the inconsequentiality of fictive creatures. Though continuing to draw on documentary sources in the next dozen chapters I wrote, I used only fictitious point-of-view characters, and each segment took on the autonomy of the short story form. Telling the larger story in these fragments, indirectly, and at a psychological remove from the actual allowed me to complete a draft of the book. In narrating the experiences of made-up cops, fictive pathologists, imagined friends, and such invented figures as a court recorder and a member of the jury, I would mostly be making mere novelistic noises from the sideline. In effect, I had given up on Pat Lowther's own experience as unimaginable.

In the spring of 1998, at the Vancouver Press Club launch of a book of my shorter fiction (*Crossing the Gulf*), I arrived early and jittery to see Beth had accepted my invitation. We talked as people started coming in, discussed "Black Rainbows" a bit, and she told me I was on the top of her list of people to write letters to. In the fall of that year, after I had spent the summer rewriting *Furry Creek*, the letter from Beth finally came, containing the remarkable passage:

Done well & lovingly: a synthesis, a rebirth, a celebration. Done insensitively, what? A tampering with the remains, or worse, dismemberment? Yikes!

It was my turn to yell "Yikes!" Beth, vulnerable to my clumsy good intentions, was brave enough to be generous.

Once more, I felt extremely unsure about what I was doing. I did not want to hurt two young women I had come to like and admire.

Hesitantly, I went back to my bulky drafts, rewriting through the fall of 1998. Often I recalled some lines from Pat Lowther:

These are our insufficient coins,
These words whose rough-hacked edges scrape the
    throat,
Scratch jagged wounds in their communicants.

Feeling too safe as a novelist, I decided to insert these autobiographical fragments into a conglomerate form that already held pages of legal transcripts, literary criticism, a cultural study of the 70s, a quasi-biography of Pat Lowther, selected letters, a *de facto* poetry anthology, and (somewhere still I hoped) a novel. Through the Christmas holidays, revising with anti-social, lunatic intensity, I at last managed to reach a place where the whole made sense to me.

Chris sent me a letter from Tofino, saying with her usual directness and humour that the characters felt realistic, her favourite one being Sunset, a cat, and she invited me to see her "bulging file" of documents and to come to the launch of her first book of poetry, *New Power*, which would be coming out in June. It pleased and reassured me that Chris's tangible voice would be heard more widely. Beth had previously told me she was thinking about resuming work on her memoirs. I had also learned that someone was writing a conventional biography of Pat Lowther, so my non-fiction novel – if published – would appear as part of a much larger, on-going, collaborative project.

In February of this year, hearing nothing at all from Beth about "Furry Creek," I called her. She said she had almost completed a second slow reading of my typescript, had a few hesitations and concerns, but strongly encouraged me to accept the publisher's offer.

Yikes!

That could have been an ending for this essay, except that I wanted to quote Susan Musgrave:

If I could foresee my own death, and know my daughters would grow up to have the dignity and the courage Pat Lowther's daughters have, I could die . . . well, with 'smiles in all my corners.'

Doing It Over

Once we've had babies
we can't stop
dreaming them; sound asleep
we grow moon bellies,
relive hospital rituals,
astonish ourselves with
blue-eyed children,
small animated mouths.

The act itself, the orgasm
of delivery
is missed; some things
no dream can recreate.
(But I didn't want anaesthetic!
I cry, dead asleep.)

Our arms keep remembering
the cradle shape,
the breasts heavy again,
the milk prickling in
to the glands
(My mother at 65
after the surgeon took
half her stomach
woke up and asked
Is the baby all right?

All our lives
swelling and germinating
in our dreams, we may
be more like plants
than we thought:
apple trees can't
forget the seasons

nor can we ever
be done with newness
but make beginnings
over and over again
in the roots of ourselves,
in the dark
between our days.

• Pat Lowther